AMAZING
•GRACIE•

Also by A. E. Cannon

CAL CAMERON BY DAY, SPIDER-MAN™ BY NIGHT
THE SHADOW BROTHERS

AMAZING
·GRACIE·

A. E. Cannon

Delacorte
Press

$\underset{C}{J}$

Published by
Delacorte Press
Bantam Doubleday Dell Publishing Group, Inc.
666 Fifth Avenue
New York, New York 10103

Library of Congress Cataloging in Publication Data

Cannon, A. E. (Ann Edwards)
    Amazing Gracie / by A. E. Cannon.
      p.   cm.
    Summary: A high school girl has a lot to deal with in her sophomore year when her beloved mother who is a victim of depression remarries, a new brother is acquired, and the family moves to Salt Lake City.
    ISBN 0-385-30487-0
    [1. Mothers and daughters—Fiction. 2. Remarriage—Fiction. 3. Depression, Mental—Fiction. 4. Moving, Household—Fiction.] I. Title.
PZ7.C17135Am   1991
[Fic]—dc20   91-6781   CIP   AC

DESIGNED BY DIANE STEVENSON/SNAP·HAUS GRAPHICS

Manufactured in the United States of America

November 1991

10 9 8 7 6 5 4 3 2

BVG

For Becky Thomas, with years of love

acknowledgments

I wish to express my deep appreciation to the following people: Wendy Lamb, for asking the right questions; Becky Price Edwards and Nan Klein, for generously sharing their professional expertise with me; Sarah Barnson, for baby-sitting my kids while I wrote; and most especially her mother, Kathy, for being the best neighbor in the universe.

AMERICAN FORK, APRIL

prologue

~~~~~~~~~~~~~~~~ ◆

If your bedroom were on fire and you had time to grab just one thing before getting out, what would it be?

That's the question Mr. Horne, the sophomore English teacher, asked our class one day.

Mike Wilson shouted out an answer from the back of the class. "I'd take Brittany Andersen!"

The class burst out laughing.

Brittany Andersen, who wore makeup in the fourth grade, turned around and said, "Shut up, geek. I wouldn't be caught dead in your bedroom."

Mr. Horne smiled a little while. "Let's say you're alone in your room." He nodded at Mike. "So be serious now. What would you grab? It would have to be something very important to you. Obviously."

"I'd grab my dog, Cuddles," Mary Ellen Myers said when Mr. Horne called on her.

3

"Cuddles?" My best friend, Sarah Macleod, whispered over my shoulder.

I laughed right out loud.

Everyone turned in their seats to stare at me.

"Okay, Gracie," Mr. Horne said, throwing a piece of chalk up in the air and catching it again, "what would *you* take?"

I blushed. "I—I don't know."

Mr. Horne sat on the edge of his desk. "Well, I'm giving you and the rest of the class a chance to think about it, because I want a one-page essay, due at the end of the hour, telling me what you'd save and why."

The class groaned and Mr. Horne grinned.

"Hey, you guys are breaking my heart," he said. "Truly."

I opened my looseleaf, pulled out a blank sheet of paper, and stared at it for a very long time. I didn't want to write about the thing I'd really take with me because I couldn't explain my choice. What could I choose instead? My radio? One of the houseplants sitting on my bedroom windowsill? My scrapbook?

I finally wrote that I'd grab my wallet because it wouldn't hurt to have some money for the things Mom and I would need if our house burned down. Mr. Horne gave my paper an A— which I thought was pretty good since I never get A's except in math and home economics.

So do you want to know what I'd really take with me?

An old Beatles album that belonged to Mom when she

was a kid. I'm not sure why I thought of it. I never listen to that record at all. I don't even know what songs are on it except for "Twist and Shout." Isn't that weird? Still, it's the one thing I'd want to save.

That is if I could.

chapter 1

~~~~~~~~~~~~~~ ◆

I wanted my mother's wedding dress to be perfect.

I wanted the seams to be straight and the hem to hang even and the collar to lay flat, but I wanted more than that, too. I wanted it to float and breathe, to swirl around her legs when she moved. I wanted it to look like this dream I had in my head. *Perfect.*

That's why I was going to make it for her myself.

She was getting married to Peter Wilding on April 26, two weeks from Saturday—plenty of time to do it right since ordinarily I can make a dress in a single day, not counting finishing touches like hooks and hems. At the moment I was waiting for her to pick me up so we could go to the mall in Orem and buy a pattern and material. I was sitting in front of American Fork High School. Our town is named after a creek which was named in response to *another* creek, Spanish Fork, that Father Escalante discovered in 1776. The Mormon pioneers who settled this place later figured Americans should get equal billing.

School had been out for thirty-five minutes.

"Hi." It was Sarah, sitting down next to me. She was wearing a short black skirt, a tight black T-shirt, black nylons, black boots, and a black leather jacket. "You know what that creep Mr. Henderson said to me?" Mr. Henderson is the sophomore health teacher.

I shook my head.

"He said that my outfit matched my roots. My roots! Can you believe he said something that rude to me?"

"He's always saying stupid stuff like that," I said. "He thinks he's David Letterman."

Sarah flattened her dyed blond hair with both hands so I could see her part. "Tell me the truth, Gracie. Can you see my roots?"

Her roots were maybe a half-inch long. "I'll come over tonight and touch them up for you." Then I added, "Why are you still here?"

Sarah shrugged as she leaned back on her elbows. "Detention Hall again. I'm b-a-a-a-d, don't you know."

Sarah and I have been best friends since the second grade and up until junior high school we were a lot alike —okay students, quiet in class, the kind of kids teachers like to have around but don't much notice. Then Sarah started to *blossom* in a strange sort of way and now everybody—the principal, the counselors, the teachers, the other kids—knows who she is.

Do you know what I think? She likes the attention.

8

Sarah has nine brothers and sisters—all of them with Bible names—and she gets lost in the crowd at home.

"You get treated like a unit," she always complains. "You have to share rooms and packs of french fries and sit on top of each other when you go some place in the car. I wish I was an only kid like you, Gracie."

Mom pulled up in her little silver Toyota and tooted the horn.

"Call me when you get home," said Sarah, "and say hello to Pete Wild Thing for me."

I pulled a face at her, then ran down the steps. When I climbed into the passenger seat, Mom's face crinkled into a big smile.

"Hey," she said, "who gave you permission to wear my blouse?"

I gave her a half-smile back. "May I wear your blouse?"

"Say please, Gracie."

"Please. Please oh please oh please."

She looked like she was giving my request a lot of serious thought. "Well, just this once . . ." she finally said. Then she burst out laughing.

Mom and I are always raiding each other's closets. We're the exact same size, and we have identical taste in clothes. Once we even gave each other the same sweater for Christmas. In fact, we have the same taste in a lot of things—food, movies, movie stars. We both love the way Mel Gibson looks, for instance. Mom and I have now watched *The Year of Living Dangerously* fourteen times, and we still look at each other and scream out loud when he shows up at the embassy reception in that tux.

Mom gunned the engine and pulled away from the curb in front of the school.

It's good to hear her laugh, I thought. Not too long ago I'd been worried again—

"Sarah sure looks scary these days," she said.

"I don't think she looks so bad."

"So how many holes does she have in her ear now?"

Whenever Sarah gets bored she has her ears pierced. Right now she has a row of little gold studs running up the outside of her left ear.

"I lose count," I said.

Mom shrugged. "It's hard to believe she's the same little girl you used to sit on the front porch and play house with. You liked baby dolls. Sarah liked Barbies."

"Because they had breasts," I said.

Mom threw back her head and laughed. "Well, anyway I'm sorry I'm late. One of the other checkers was late and Glen asked me to stay an extra hour. I hate it when he does that to me."

"Just tell him you can't," I said.

She shrugged.

"Your problem is that you're too nice," I said. "You never say no. Never. You just smile and say, 'I'd be happy to.' You gotta stop letting people walk all over you."

"Well, I won't be ringing up groceries for much longer anyway," she said happily.

I stared at her in disbelief. "You're quitting?" Mom has

worked at Albertson's Market ever since my dad died when I was four.

She coughed and her cheeks went pink. "Well, not right this instant," she said. Her words came in a rush, and I had this very strong feeling there was something she wasn't telling me. "Pete really thinks he can make a go of his Americalife business if he pursues it full-time, and I think he can, too."

Americalife is a line of powders and tablets that are supposed to make you "fit and trim—the easy, natural way!" You can't buy them in a store. You have to buy them from Americalife distributors like Pete. If you want to sell them, "you can *become a distributor, too!*"

"Multilevel marketing!" Pete says like he's trying out for head cheerleader. "It's the marketing trend of the future!"

I snorted out loud. "Pete has a pretty good job at Geneva Steel right now."

"Well, the man who introduced Pete to Americalife while he was living in southern California has made over one hundred thousand dollars in one year," Mom said.

I didn't say anything.

"It's the truth," said Mom.

"Oh right."

"Pete doesn't want to work at a steel mill for the rest of his life," Mom said, her voice climbing a little, "and I don't blame him. He's always wanted to run his own business. It's been a dream of his for a long time."

I rolled my eyes.

11

"Don't be such a know-it-all, Gracie," Mom said.

I glared at her. "I am not a know-it-all!"

I looked out the window and read road signs while a red flush crept up my neck.

"Oh, come on," Mom said after a while. "Don't be angry." She reached for one of my hands and gave it a squeeze. "Okay?"

I didn't answer.

"Okay, Gracie? Let's not ruin our time together."

Why did I act like this? I go along just fine, taking everything in stride, and then suddenly I fall to pieces over the littlest thing. I get mad and yell and say things I have to apologize for after. If I could change one thing about myself, it would be my temper. My stupid awful temper.

"I'm sorry," I said finally, even though being called a know-it-all still stung.

Mom gave my hand another squeeze. "Nothing to be sorry about, Baby. I just hate to fight. You know how much I hate to fight."

The tires of the car hummed beneath us. Mom flipped on the radio to a country-western station.

"I love this song," she said. It was a Reba McEntire tune. Mom listened carefully, then sang the words of the chorus on the second time through. Her voice sounded thick and smoky, with something a little sad behind it.

The sadness made me a little nervous.

A woman carrying a couple of plastic bags walked up to us as we got out of the car in the University Mall parking lot. Her clothes didn't match, and they were so dirty I could smell them.

"Excuse me," she said. "You ladies got some money you can loan me? I'm lookin' for bus fare. Gotta get home, take care of my kids."

"I bet we can help you out," Mom said. She opened her purse and rummaged around, frowning. "I don't have any change—"

"Even a nickel. A nickel would be great."

"Oh!" Mom's face brightened. "Here we go!" She pulled out a ten-dollar bill and handed it to the woman.

"Thanks. I mean it."

"Take care," Mom said as we walked away.

"That was a ten-dollar bill you gave her," I said.

"I got paid today," Mom said.

"I bet she doesn't really have any kids."

"Maybe, maybe not." Mom shrugged. "I try not to judge people too hard. You never know what's happened in their lives."

The fabric store in the mall is huge with lots of bolts of bright crisp cloth. As we walked through the store to the table where the pattern books are kept, I ran my finger across the bolts of cloth because I just love the way different fabrics—satin, velvet, denim, silk, flannel—feel against my skin.

Mom and I thumbed through the pattern books for nearly an hour before we found the right pattern.

"Look," I said, barely breathing when I saw it. "*This* would be perfect."

Mom squinted as she looked over at my book. A slow smile started to spread across her face. "Yes. Yes, you're right. What color do you think, Gracie?"

"Rose," I said. "Definitely rose."

Mom nodded.

"Let's see," I said, "it says you need five and one-half yards but I bet I could lay it out so that we'd only need to get five and three-eighths."

Mom looked up from the book and started to laugh a little. "Five and three-eighths?" she asked.

"Every little bit helps," I said defensively.

Mom put her hand on the back of my neck. "I know it does, Baby. I know it does." She sighed. "Maybe one day you and I and Pete won't have to worry about money anymore. Wouldn't that be nice?"

It certainly would be, I thought, but I wasn't counting on it. Frankly, my new stepfather-to-be, Pete Wilding, didn't seem like the kind of guy destined to make a million dollars. He's a big, slow-moving man with red hair and rusty freckles. It's the freckles that get me. They make him look like an oversized kid—that and the way he dresses. He wears running shoes, with Velcro strips instead of shoelaces, for instance, and faded old T-shirts from Seaworld featuring Shamu the Killer Whale. You wonder how he dares to wear stuff like that in public.

"I have a surprise for you, Gracie," Mom said. "Pete told me today that he wants you to have a new dress for the wedding, too. A nice one. His treat."

I almost jumped, hearing Pete's name spoken at the same time I was thinking about him.

"Tell you what," Mom said. "Let's finish here, then go find you a dress. Okay?"

I smiled and nodded.

We found the dress—a blue Laura Ashley jumper that still cost fifty times more than it was worth even though it was on sale. But when I put it on, I knew it was the dress I wanted.

Mom and I stood in the dressing room together, looking at my reflection in the mirror.

"Oh, Baby," she whispered, "it's *so* beautiful. You look just like you're wearing a piece of the sky!"

I laughed out loud because I had just been thinking the same thing. Mom and I do that sometimes—think the same thought at the same time.

"We really *do* look alike, don't we?" she said, smiling at the sight of us together. "Everybody says we do."

I had to agree. We're both short and small, with long permed black hair, dark eyes, and fair skin that always burns in the sun.

"The only difference is that I'm getting wrinkles," Mom said.

"You do not have wrinkles."

"Yes I do." She made a tight grin into the mirror, then pointed at tiny webs of lines at the corners of her eyes.

"Get out of here," I said, and her face relaxed into its regular smile.

We looked at each other and were quiet for a moment.

"You're my best friend, Gracie girl," she finally whispered. "Thank you for such a perfect day."

Pete was sitting on the living room couch, eating a bowl of his favorite cold cereal—Frankenberry—and watching *Family Feud* on television.

"Watermelon!" he yelled at the screen. "Say watermelon!"

He looked up and smiled at us. "They're asking what things people take on picnics."

Pete's hair was wet and his face and neck were scrubbed clean. He'd stopped on his way home from work at Geneva Steel, taken a shower, and changed into the set of clean clothes he keeps at our house. He doesn't actually live with us yet, but sometimes it feels like it.

I felt my face go red. I'd washed out one of my bras before school that morning, then draped it over the shower rod to dry. That meant Pete would have seen it. Worse. He would have had to *touch* it, pick it up and put it someplace else.

I wanted to crawl in a hole.

There was clapping and cheering on the television. "Yes!" said Pete. "I knew it was watermelon." He sighed happily. "This is Sinjian's favorite game show." Sinjian is Pete's six-year-old son who lives in California with Pete's ex-wife Lily. I've seen a million pictures of him, but I've never met him.

Mom walked over to Pete and planted a big kiss on the

top of his slick red hair. I looked away as he folded an arm around her waist.

"I'm glad you're here," Mom said.

"Gracie," Pete said. "I got a little present for you."

I faced him, my cheeks still pink from thinking about my bra. He gave Mom a squeeze, then got up as slow as a bear from the couch. He flipped off the TV set and picked up a paper bag sitting next to it.

"Here." He handed the bag to me.

I opened it and pulled out a dress.

"For the wedding," Pete said with a big smile.

It had an eyelet bodice, a flowered skirt, a purple sash, and a black velveteen bolero. It was the ugliest dress I had ever seen.

"But Pete—"

"It's—it's wonderful. Isn't it, Gracie," Mom said in a voice that was too loud. I could feel her eyes, silently warning me.

"I told your Mom I wanted you to have something real nice, and when I saw this in the window, I knew I had to get it for you." Pete looked as pleased as a kid with a new trophy. "They had to take it off the mannequin and everything for me because they only had one left."

I just kept thinking about the Laura Ashley jumper, neatly folded and wrapped carefully in tissue. The beautiful Laura Ashley jumper that looked like it had been cut from the sky.

"What do you say to Pete, Gracie," Mom said, her voice a little higher than usual.

17

I didn't say anything. She was treating me like a little kid, reminding me to say please and thank you. The room grew so quiet I could hear the ticking of my own watch.

Pete shifted his weight from one foot to the other. "If you don't like it—"

"It's nice," I said. "Thank you."

Pete let out a deep breath, then laughed. "Whew! You had me all worried there for a second."

Mom gave me a nervous smile.

"I'll go hang this up now," I said, looking down at the carpet. I turned and ran.

When I got to my room, I threw the dress on the floor, flopped onto my bed, and buried my face in my pillow. The cotton pillowcase felt cool against my cheeks. I swallowed hard, then rolled on my side and grabbed the radio sitting on my nightstand. I turned it on loud.

She wanted me to *lie*. She wanted me to stand right there in the middle of the living room with a straight face and say, oh thank you, thank you, Pete, for that extremely gorgeous dress you tore off some mannequin which is now standing naked in some store window somewhere.

I turned up the radio even louder.

There was a knock at my door. Which I ignored.

Another knock.

"Gracie?" Mom opened it and poked her head inside. "Can I come in?"

I gave a nod that could have meant either yes or no. She slipped in as quiet as a shadow.

As soon as she spotted the dress on the floor, she stooped over, picked it up, shook it gently straight, and hung it in my closet.

"I hate it," I said. "I really hate it!"

Mom flitted nervously around the room, pretending to straighten things on my dresser even though everything was already in place. "Pete was only trying to be nice."

"He should have asked me what I thought about it before he bought it. I don't like surprises."

She looked at me quickly, then glanced away, and right away I had that strange feeling again she wasn't telling me everything.

"Please. Let's not fight—"

"We can't keep both dresses, Mom!"

"Sure we can, Baby." She was pleading with me. "Don't talk so loud. Pete will hear."

"So!" We stared at each other until she looked away. "We cannot keep both dresses. Since I am the only person around here who ever tries to balance the checkbook, I know for a fact that you can't afford to buy me a Laura Ashley jumper. I thought Pete already gave you the money."

"He was going to tonight," she said miserably, "but he found your dress instead."

I snorted. "I don't know what you see in that guy, Mom. He's a big clown. A loser."

19

She froze. "If you ever say something like that about Pete to me again, I'll slap you," she said in a growl.

I gulped. Mom never gets really mad, especially not at me.

"I'm—I'm sorry."

Mom let out a breath and her shoulders went limp. She smiled a little.

"Can I sit down?" she asked.

I nodded, and she sat on the foot of my bed.

"You don't know Pete very well yet," she said quietly, looking at the wall. "After all he's only been in your life since he moved back here from Los Angeles, and I'm sure it's really hard for you to get used to having somebody new in our family."

"It's not that, Mom." I rolled over on my back and sighed. "It's just that things have happened so fast. He's only been here for two months." It's embarrassing, I wanted to say, to have your mother get engaged on a third date with some guy.

"I knew the very first time he asked me out that he was right for me."

I didn't say anything.

"Baby, I've known Pete since we were kids. We went to school together—elementary, junior high, high school. He was kind of shy—"

Shy? Pete never stops talking and telling the kind of dopey jokes you read in joke books.

"—and big for his age although he never was very good at sports. Sometimes the other guys teased him about that, but he was always nice. To everybody. A thing like that means more to you when you get older."

She looked straight at me. "He loves me. He knows about—about that time when you were little, and he still loves me."

It was my turn to stare at the wall.

"Everything's going to be so much *better* now, Gracie," she said, her eyes gleaming. "I'm gonna have some of the things I've always dreamed about, you know? Security. Companionship. I won't be so lonely anymore."

I felt like a little pin just pricked my heart. Lonely?

"I feel like I'm getting a brand new start. I'm not even the same person anymore!"

How could she be lonely with me here all the time? I never knew she felt that way.

Mom grabbed my hand and gave it a hard squeeze. "I'm so happy, Gracie, and I want you to be happy for me, too. Okay?"

I blinked. Well, that's all I ever wanted—for her to be happy.

Didn't she *know* that by now?

chapter 2

~~~~~~~~~~~~~~~~ ◆

My mom isn't like other moms.

Sarah would say she's too pretty. "I'm never having babies," Sarah likes to tell me, "because then you get fat. Except for your mom, Gracie. I promise she looks twenty years old."

She does look young for her age, and in some ways she acts young, too. She listens to the radio turned way up loud, buys her clothes at the same places I do, reads my magazines, dots the "i" in her name with a circle, has a diet Coke and a bag of Cheez Doodles for lunch.

Sarah's mom would never eat like that. She cooks three meals a day. Oatmeal, toast, and orange juice for breakfast. Sandwiches, apple slices, and carrot sticks for lunch. Beef, potatoes, homemade rolls, green beans she bottled out of the family garden, and Jell-O salad for dinner. On Sundays she makes a big sheet cake, chocolate or spice. They're not fancy meals, but you can tell she's trying her best to feed her family healthy food on not a lot of money.

I wish Mom ate better. I *know* it would help her to stay well. Because sometimes she gets—sick.

It started happening when I was four, the same year my dad was killed in an industrial accident. This is a horrible thing to admit, but I can hardly remember him now, even when I look at old pictures of him smiling and holding me on his lap. It's like he never really existed, although every now and then I'll brush by some man in a store or on the street, and the smell of his cologne will make me stop short.

After he died, Mom got a job as a checker at the grocery store. I stayed with Sarah's family during the day until Mom picked me up. After work we did everything together—played, took walks, watched TV, ran errands, drove over to the mall in Orem. Before she finally bought a washer and dryer we used to go to the Laundromat once a week where she let me put dimes in the vending machine to buy little packets of sweet-smelling soap.

When I went to bed at night, she fixed me a glass of chocolate milk and rubbed the back of my neck so I wouldn't have bad dreams. Sometimes she read books to me, the kind you buy from spinning racks at grocery stores, but mostly she sang songs. Songs from the radio, songs from my dad's old records, songs she knew when she was a kid herself—even the ones with silly words like "Glory glory hallelujah, Teacher hit me with a ruler."

I loved it when she sang to me. I loved her voice, the

way she sat on my bed, the way the moon coming through my window made the crown of her head shine. I thought she looked like a mermaid sitting on the edge of the sand. She had *such* long hair then.

But sometimes she'd start to fade away. She'd come home from work and lie down on the couch and not get up again until it was time to fix me dinner or put me to bed. She still sang to me, but she sounded far away, even though we were together in the same room. I'd notice how thin everything about her was getting—her voice, her face, her arms. I could see the veins running through her hands like little blue tubes.

Then in a few weeks she would be herself again, talking and laughing and kissing the top of my head.

Once when I was about seven she didn't get better. I first realized something very bad was happening when she stopped coming into my room at night.

"Will you sing me a song, Mom?" I'd call from my bed.

"Just a minute, Baby," she'd say.

But she'd still be lying on our couch in the living room, newspapers strewn around the floor, watching the flash of black-and-white pictures on the television, when I'd finally fall asleep.

The next morning, I'd find her on the couch, still wearing the clothes she had on the night before.

She also stopped fixing meals. I ate big lunches at Sarah's house and figured out that I could fix cold cereal or toast for myself at home whenever I got hungry, although

I had to call Mom on the phone to remind her to bring stuff from the store.

After a while she stopped going to work.

"Pull the drapes and take the phone off the hook for me, Baby," she'd say in a flat voice. So I'd lay the receiver on its side and listen to the signal scream like a magpie through the dark house until the line went dead.

She didn't talk very much to me anymore. She didn't laugh at my jokes or tell me to change my underwear or scold me whenever I drew pictures all over my arms with a ballpoint pen. Instead, she lay on the couch.

I didn't want to go to bed at night because I was afraid when I woke up, she'd be gone. Just like that.

One day when Mom was lying down and I was in the kitchen figuring out how to fry an egg, someone knocked on our front door.

"Cynthia?" It was Mrs. Macleod.

She knocked again, harder and longer. "Cynthia!" Her voice was sharp now.

I didn't know what to do.

"It's okay, Gracie," Mom said softly. "You can open the door."

Mrs. Macleod, who was bouncing one of her babies on a hip, took one step into our house.

"Cynthia, I just got a call from the store—" She stopped talking, stopped jostling the baby, practically stopped breathing as she looked around the living room. I started to see things through her eyes—piles of unread newspapers, dirty clothes in the corner, unmatched shoes scattered across the floor, empty cups with milk rings.

"Oh, Cynthia—"

The baby wailed.

I could feel shame spread from my stomach all the way to my fingers and toes and to the top of my head. I started to scurry around the room, bumping into the furniture while trying to pick up stray papers from the floor. Blood was pounding in my ears.

"Honey, honey," Mrs. Macleod said to me. "Come here."

Shaking, I walked toward her. She put an arm around me and pulled me close so that my face was buried in her big bosom. "Don't worry about any of that right now. Why don't you go to your room while me and your mom talk for a while. Okay?" She kissed me quick on the cheek and gave me a gentle push.

I raced to my room but left the door opened just a crack so I could hear.

"Glen's been trying to call you but he keeps getting a busy signal," Mrs. Macleod said. "He said you was supposed to go back to work this morning. I said I thought you was still on vacation."

"I'm going to lose my job now. I wish I could die."

Die? I went completely cold.

"No you don't," Mrs. Macleod said sharply. "Don't you ever say that again."

Mom started to cry.

"Now you listen here, Cynthia," said Mrs. Macleod. "You've got plenty of people that care about you. Do you understand me?"

Mom cried and cried.

What happened next is that Mrs. Macleod called her husband. He came straight home from work to take Mom to the doctor, who said that she was depressed. *Depressed.* I said the word over and over so I could understand what it meant. He also gave her a prescription for some pills.

But she didn't get better. Who knows why? So she finally went to the state hospital in Provo, and I stayed with the Macleods for a month. It felt like an entire year. I talked to her on the telephone almost every night, but she told me I couldn't see her. Not yet.

Sarah said we were twins now and that we had to change our names to Vanessa Dee and Valerie Dawn. She thought we were having a slumber party that never ended, but I was *so* happy the day Mr. Macleod brought Mom back to American Fork.

Sarah and I were playing Barbies in Sarah's bedroom.

"Gracie?" Mom was standing in the doorway.

I paused. "What—what happened to your hair?"

She ran her hand across the top of her head. "I had it cut. Easier to take care of that way, you know."

Her hair looked like a curly little hat that didn't fit.

"Do you want me to grow it back?" Mom smiled.

27

I nodded, and she opened her arms. I threw down my Barbie and ran straight to her.

"Let's go home, Baby," she said, hugging me hard.

That was the worst time, but it wasn't the last. We'd go along just fine, then suddenly there would be these little *signs* again. She didn't eat. She didn't sleep. She didn't comb her hair or hang up her clothes.

She cried.

Usually she managed to make it to work, but then she'd come home and lie on the couch. Whenever I saw her there, looking at the TV without really watching it, my stomach turned over.

Here we go again.

Sometimes I could almost figure out the reason she got sick—something didn't turn out the way she expected, she was tired of her job, she stopped taking her medicine once she felt better and then got sick all over again.

But other times it hit for no reason at all—straight out of the blue like a snowstorm in summer.

I keep looking for the thing that's going to make her well, and I'm going to find it.

I really am.

chapter 3

~~~~~~~~~~~~~~~~~~~ ◆

Later on that night when Pete asked me if I wanted to go with him and Mom to get hamburgers, I said no because I was still mad. Mom could say whatever she wanted to, but I knew we couldn't keep both dresses. In fact, I'd already made plans to catch the bus for Orem after school so I could return the Laura Ashley jumper.

After they pulled away from the house in Pete's pickup, I went to the Macleods to touch up Sarah's roots. Her four-year-old sister, Rachel, met me at the front door and zapped me with her toy laser gun.

"You're totally dead, Gracie," she said.

I just love everything about Rachel—her white dandelion-fuzz hair, her clothes that don't match because she won't let anybody dress her, her voice. Rachel has a loud deep voice which sounds very strange coming out of a person her size. Her big brothers call her Donkey.

"When are you coming to live at my house?" I teased her, smiling.

"Never."

"But I'm so lonely, Rachel, and I want a little sister just like you. We'll have slumber parties and play beauty parlor every night."

She vaporized me again.

"You can even have all my old Barbies, Rachel. I promise."

This made her think.

"Gracie?" Mrs. Macleod called from the kitchen. "Come on in here."

"I'll move in to your house tomorrow," Rachel called after me.

Mrs. Macleod was standing at the kitchen sink. "Sarah's not here. She took off about fifteen minutes ago, mad as a hornet at her dad about something. I can hardly wait until that kid starts coming to her senses again. But I'm glad you're here because I know you'll appreciate this as much as I do. Take a look."

I joined her at the sink and saw a collander full of bright green asparagus.

"Dale picked it for me on his way home from work. Saw it growing next to a ditch bank. My dad used to say a person should eat asparagus three times a day when it's in season because it's a gift straight from God. My kids sure don't feel that way, though." She laughed. "I didn't even bother to fix it for dinner, but now that you're here, I'll boil it up so you and me can share it."

I made a move to help her, but she pushed me away. "I know you can't stand to sit still, but I want you to take it easy. Sit down, Gracie."

I took a seat at the picnic table where the Macleods eat and looked around. The kitchen overflowed with things —dishes, boxes of cereal and rice, school art projects stuck on the fridge with masking tape, heaps of sweat-shirts and shoes in the corner by the door. Like the whole house, it was too small for twelve people, but I always liked the way it felt—cozy and full of warm smells.

I also liked watching Mrs. Macleod drop the asparagus spears into a kettle of boiling water. It really surprised me when I first realized that Mrs. Macleod is about the same age as my mom. She looks older—maybe because she's a little heavy or because she doesn't care very much about clothes or even because my mom looks so young. But when I see her do things like peel potatoes or talk to one of her kids, I always think she's pretty.

Mrs. Macleod lifted the lid from the kettle and a cloud of fragrant steam escaped. "What have you been up to today?"

"Me and Mom went to the mall to buy some material for a wedding dress."

"Have fun?"

"Yes," I answered slowly. "We probably won't have many more days alone together."

I winced when I remembered her words: *"I won't be so lonely anymore."*

Mrs. Macleod gave me a sharp look. "Well now, does that make you feel bad?"

I started to shake my head, then ended up shrugging my shoulders instead. "It's just been us two for such a long time—"

Danny chased Josh into the kitchen, hitting him with a plastic baseball bat.

"Stop that!" snapped Mrs. Macleod, yanking the bat from Danny's hand. "Go do your homework right now." She hustled them out, then sat down next to me.

The kitchen grew so quiet I could hear the water boil.

"Gracie, Gracie. I been carrying you around in my heart these past few months. I'm sure things haven't been easy for you lately—but then they never have been," she finished in a quiet voice.

I looked at the plastic tablecloth.

"You know I keep a list inside my head of all the questions I plan on asking God when I die, like for instance why can't men be pregnant just once so they'd all know how it feels."

I laughed.

Mrs. Macleod smiled, then grew serious. "And I'd also like to know why some babies don't have enough to eat and why some old people can't have their dignity and why there's got to be a thing as mean as what happens to your mother. I can't stand the way she's had to suffer." Mrs. Macleod's cheeks were pink and her voice shook. "You know I've really tried to understand it. Whenever I see an article in the newspaper or a magazine about depression I read it but I still don't know *exactly* what causes it. Some people say it's the way you're put together physically and other people say it's the type of personality you are. I don't think anybody knows for sure."

The room felt suddenly hot and my stomach was starting to roll.

"I—I was worried about her a little while ago," Mrs. Macleod said, "right before Pete came back to town."

So. I wasn't the only one who'd noticed that she had been a little off.

"Did she go see the doctor?" Mrs. Macleod asked.

I shrugged helplessly. "I don't know. I never know. When I try to ask her anything about—her problem, she just shuts me out."

Mrs. Macleod put her hand over mine.

"Sometimes I can tell she's been to the doctor, because she seems a little happier," I went on. "She eats more, sleeps better, laughs, so I figure that she's on some kind of medication that's helping her. But I never really know for sure because she hides her pills. Also, I don't think she always takes them—"

"She's got to keep taking them," Mrs. Macleod said, "even when she starts feeling better or she'll wind up where she started from. It's like my little kids and their earaches in the winter. I gotta give them the whole bottle of Septra even though they're up and running around the next day."

"Why doesn't she take care of herself!" I blurted. "It's so frustrating."

Mrs. Macleod reached up, brushed a strand of hair from my forehead. "I know, I know. Sometimes I want to march right over there and take charge, but I can't. I'm just a neighbor." She paused, then said softly, "You know what I think sometimes? That your mom is ashamed. Having to go away like she did when she was such a young woman, leave her baby here with us, face talk when she got back, from people who don't know anything. I think it made her feel like such a failure that she can't even face the problem now."

I swallowed hard.

"But I think Pete can help now, honey. Dale and I are so happy your mom has found a kind man."

"I don't know how much he really knows—" My voice trailed. "Besides, I think he's a little flakey. Did you know he's going to quit his job at Geneva so he can sell Americalife full-time?"

Mrs. Macleod blinked.

"See what I mean?" I said. *And there's more, too.* I wanted to say. *I can feel it. It's just that nobody's telling me.*

"I had no idea Pete was quitting." Mrs. Macleod stood up suddenly, walked over to the stove, and lifted the kettle from the burner without using hot pads. "Damn!"

"You owe me a dollar, Mom," said Luke as he strolled

into the kitchen. "You said you had to pay a dollar any time we caught you swearing."

"Good things can come from change," said Mrs. Macleod, ignoring Luke.

But she didn't look too convinced.

chapter 4

"This is how they do it in France." Sarah took a drag on her cigarette, then blew the smoke out her nose instead of her mouth.

We were standing in the church parking lot, waiting for Mom's reception to start. "You're going to be in a lot of trouble if somebody tells your dad," I said. He's the leader of the congregation.

"What's he gonna do? Give me the chair?" Sarah blew smoke at me. "Stop acting like a person's mother, Gracie."

Sarah never worries about anything. Today she took her dad's pickup without asking first, then accidentally drove it into an irrigation ditch. She thought it was hilarious.

The church door opened. Mrs. Johnson walked outside and sniffed the air like a bird dog. "Are you girls smoking out here?"

Sarah took a drag. "No," she said.

Mrs. Johnson gave Sarah a look. "Sarah Macleod, you ought to know better than to smoke them things so close to the House of the Lord." I could feel my cheeks go pink. "Gracie, your mother's looking for you."

I smoothed down my flowered skirt. No more Laura Ashley jumper.

"Anybody ever tell you that you look just like her?" Mrs. Johnson asked.

"Sometimes."

"Bet you sing as pretty as she does, too. Now hurry on inside." She scowled at Sarah again before she left.

"Hey, I would *kill* the person who told me I looked like my mother," said Sarah as she stubbed out her cigarette. "Justifiable homicide."

Mrs. Macleod is maybe thirty or forty pounds overweight. She used to be skinny, she says, before she had ten kids.

Sarah found some breath mints in her purse and popped them in her mouth, then said, "Your mother, on the other hand, is pure gorgeous."

"Do you think her dress looks okay?" It didn't turn out exactly the way I wanted it to.

Sarah rolled her eyes. "I told you already it looks just fine. Let's go inside."

A few ladies from the congregation were still arranging silk flowers in baskets from K mart when Sarah and I walked into the gym where the reception was being held. The flowers were going to be centerpieces for the tables where guests would eat strawberry parfaits and nuts from paper cups. Three little girls in the corner were trying to play their violins. The music sounded exactly like cats fighting.

I sighed. On the one hand it was very nice of Mr. Macleod to let Mom and Pete have a reception here even though they don't go to church. On the other, the whole thing was just so tacky—the fake flowers, the big pink plastic bows hanging from the basketball hoops at each end of the gym, the folding chairs with chipped paint lined up like bleachers against the wall.

I realize that this is usually how receptions are done around here—church recreation halls can hold lots of friends and big families—but when I get married I will *not* have a reception in a gym.

"Gracie!" It was Mom. She waved, then started toward me and Sarah.

"The pleats don't hang right," I said.

Sarah groaned.

Mom kissed me on the cheek when she reached us, then slipped her arm through mine.

"Hello, Sarah," she said, smiling. Mom is practically the only adult left who treats Sarah like a normal person.

Sarah smiled back, only she looked like she was sneering. It was the black lipstick.

"You look really beautiful, Baby."

"No I don't," I said. "I hate this dress."

Mom's face clouded a little, but she kept smiling. "She does so look pretty, doesn't she, Sarah."

Sarah curled her upper lip. "She looks like that girl

who lived in the Alps with her grandfather—Heidi What's-her-face."

Mom shook her head. "You two." She turned to me. "There's a corsage for you in the kitchen just like mine. Go put it on, Baby, and then you and me and Pete can have our pictures taken."

I felt my stomach sink straight to my shoes.

"I don't want to have my picture taken, Mom."

How could I explain to her that I didn't want to pose with Pete in front of a camera like I was really his daughter, making fake smiles for some photographer? I hardly knew anything about him, and suddenly we were supposed to be a family.

"Gracie, please—"

I could feel my face go pink all over again.

"Mom—"

She looked hurt.

I quickly folded my arms. "Fine. Okay."

"There you are, Cynthia!" Pete came up behind us. He put his arm around Mom's narrow shoulders and pulled her close to him. She cuddled up to him like he was her great big teddy bear.

"Hi, Gracie!"

Pete talks in exclamation points.

"Nice suit," said Sarah out of the side of her mouth.

He looked down at his borrowed brown suit—it was a couple of sizes too small—then smiled at Sarah.

"Oh! Thanks!"

People were starting to drift into the gym.

"Pictures will have to wait," said Pete. "Let's say hi to everybody." He and Mom left, their arms draped around each other.

"Young love," said Sarah. "Isn't it sweet?"

I pulled a face at her.

"Let's eat," said Sarah.

We sat down at one of the tables with the fake flowers and Sarah's eleven-year-old sister, Elizabeth, brought us our refreshments.

She wrinkled up her nose. "You've been smoking again, Sarah."

"No duh," said Sarah.

"I'm telling Dad."

Sarah pinched Elizabeth on the arm, then said, "I'm sneaking into your bedroom tonight with a pair of scissors so I can cut all your hair off after you're asleep."

"Liar!" said Elizabeth. But she looked scared.

"Be glad you don't have any brothers and sisters, Gracie," Sarah said after Elizabeth left. "Can I have your cashews?"

I watched the people coming into the gym while Sarah picked through my nut cup. There were guys who worked with Pete at the steel mill, their hair clean and slicked back, a little uncomfortable in Sunday suits. And there were people from the store where Mom worked as a checker, including Danny. Danny is a forty-year-old re-tarded man who bags groceries and brings empty shopping carts in from the parking lot.

40

Mom threw her arms around Danny, then pulled away and listened to him like he was the only person in the room, even though there was a line of people waiting to shake her hand.

"Your mom is *so* sweet." Sarah was watching Mom, too. "Maybe that's why she's marrying Pete. She feels sorry for him."

"Give me a break."

Sarah pulled a face and I shrugged.

"I don't get it either," I said.

I saw Mr. Messick go through the line. He owns a small farm not far from where Mom and I live, and in the fall one acre is nothing but pumpkins. I love how fat and orange they glow in early October when the sun hits them first thing in the morning.

Mr. Messick is going to help me start some flower gardens in May when the weather warms up—a small one in front, a huge one in back. I love flowers. I think they make a house look finished. Like a *home.* He waved when he saw me.

"Have you ever noticed how rough his hands are?" Sarah asked. "And his thumbnails! They're like tortoise shells they're so thick. They give me the creeps!" She shivered.

I laughed although I like Mr. Messick's hands. They look like hands that work and take care of things.

"You're so quiet tonight," said Sarah.

I dipped a spoon into my strawberry parfait. "Well, it's

not every day my mom gets married. I'm still getting used to the idea."

Sarah squinted at Pete and Mom again. "Do you ever think about them doing it?"

"Sarah!"

"It gives me the hyper-willies to think about my own parents doing it."

Pete had his arm around Mom's shoulder and she nestled into his side. A perfect fit. Suddenly I felt hollow inside.

"Everything's different," I said slowly.

Sarah leaned across the table. "Hey! I just thought of something, Gracie. This marriage is going to be the *best* thing that ever happened. You aren't going to have to stick around the house anymore. Your mom's got Pete to help her now. You'll be free. We'll go to dances every night. We'll meet guys. We'll take Pete's car—"

"And drive it straight into a ditch."

Sarah laughed so loud that her chair began to tip.

Mom spotted us and waved.

"You gotta admit she looks happy, Gracie."

"She certainly does." Have you ever felt two different emotions at the same time? Pete Wilding made me feel grateful for making Mom happy, but something else, too. Resentful.

A lady with flowing red hair walked through the door. She wore a violet tie-dyed dress, a crystal necklace, and sandals. At her side was a little boy. He had on a pair of sunglasses that were too big for him and a glove on one hand.

"Who is *that*?" said Sarah.

I knew exactly who they were.

chapter 5

~~~~~~~~~~~~~~~~~~~~ ◆

"It's Pete's ex-wife and their kid," I
said. "Pete has a million pictures of him."

"So you *do* have a little brother," said Sarah.

I hadn't thought of it that way. "A little *stepbrother.*"

"Now you can be just like that sickening family on
reruns," said Sarah. "You know who I mean. The guy
with the sons who marries the lady with the girls. They
just all lo-o-o-ve each other to death. They love the
housekeeper, too. *The Brady Bunch!* That's it." She
started to sing. "Here's the story of a lovely lady—"

"I didn't know they were coming in from California," I
said. "I wonder if Mom knows?"

A little knot formed in my stomach. How would she
react?

Mom stiffened when she saw Lily, but she smiled anyway and held out her hand.

The knot in my stomach tightened.

Pete blushed when his old wife put her arms around him to give him a hug.

"Now *that* is very weird," said Sarah, watching the whole thing. "I thought divorced people were supposed to hate each other."

"I think she must be kind of strange," I agreed. "She believes in past lives. Things like that."

"Really?" Sarah was holding a lock of her hair in front of her face, looking for split ends.

"Yeah. Pete said she thinks she used to be Amelia Earhart."

"Hmm," said Sarah. "I wonder who I was."

Mom was bent down on her knees so that she and Pete's kid were looking straight into each others' eyes. She asked him questions, then nodded at his answers as though they were the most interesting things she'd ever heard.

Pete gave his kid a hug, then pointed at me and Sarah. The boy turned around to look at us. Pete said something to him, then gave him a little push. He started dragging slowly across the floor toward us, pouting.

He stopped at the table.

"You can sit here with us if you want to," I said.

He pulled out a chair like he was doing me and Sarah a great big favor and sat down.

I knew that he was six, but he looked younger because he was so small. With his olive skin and huge hazel eyes, he was pretty enough to be a girl, in spite of his missing front teeth and the goofy way he was wearing his hair.

He had a long punk tail in back while the shorter hair on the top of his head stood straight up.

"So what's your name?" asked Sarah.

"Michael Jackson."

Sarah looked at me over his head and went cross-eyed.

"Get outta here. You are not Michael Jackson," she said.

He thought about this for a while.

"Well, I'm his best friend," he said finally. "He even gave me this glove." He waved the hand with the glove on it right under Sarah's nose.

"His name is Sinjian," I said.

"How did you know?" he asked, very surprised.

"Lucky guess," I joked. He still looked confused. "Your dad told me. Just like he probably told you my name is Gracie."

Sinjian slumped back in his chair like he was completely bored. "Yeah," he said. "That sure is a stupid name."

So this was my new little brother?

"How come your hair does that?" asked Sarah. "Are you wearing hairspray or something?"

Sinjian didn't say anything.

"Don't wear hairspray here because you'll get beat up. Okay?"

He thought about this, too.

"Well, I know karate," Sinjian said.

Sarah started to laugh.

"I do so!" Sinjian started shouting. The people sitting at the next table turned to look us.

"Shh," I said.

"This is *exactly* what you need in your life, Gracie," Sarah said. "More crazy people."

For a second I thought I might stop breathing.

"Oh, Gracie," Sarah whispered. "I'm sorry. You know I didn't mean anything by that—"

"It's okay," I said in a tiny voice that was nothing like my own.

"You're Gracie, aren't you?"

It was Pete's ex-wife.

"That's right," I said. "And this is my friend, Sarah Macleod."

Sarah scowled.

"I'm Lily," she said, smiling brightly and pulling her chair up so close to mine it made me feel uncomfortable in the same way you do when someone you've never met takes the seat right next to you at a movie theater.

"Pete said not to buy a present," said Lily, her face close to mine, "but I did anyway. It's the medicine woman trilogy by Lynne Andrews."

I blinked.

"You know," said Lily, *"Jaguar Woman, Star Woman.* Pretty interesting stuff."

"Oh," I said. What Mom and Pete really needed was a new blender.

"Gracie says you used to be Amelia Earhart," said Sarah.

Lily laughed. "I'll bet Pete told you that," she said to me.

I nodded, embarrassed that Sarah had even brought up the subject.

"He's making fun of me," she said, "because I believe in reincarnation."

"I think that's really neat." Sarah's eyes were shining. "I mean it. I want to know who I was."

I snorted.

"You're like Pete," said Lily with a little smile.

"It's just that it's so stupid," I blurted out. "People who believe in that stuff always think they were somebody famous. They never think they were secretaries or waitresses."

Nobody said anything. Why couldn't I just keep my mouth shut?

"Well," said Lily finally, "Sinjian here is really excited about living with you guys."

I stammered. "With me?"

Lily's light laugh made me think of wind chimes. "And with Pete and Cynthia, too, of course."

Sinjian was slipping further and further down in his seat. Any minute now and he would be on the floor.

"Sinjian is going to live with us?" I knew I sounded stupid, but I couldn't help myself.

Lily was still smiling that copper bright smile of hers, but she was starting to look as bewildered as I felt.

"Well, yes. For the spring and summer anyway. I'm

moving to New Mexico to study under this new teacher—"

And I don't want to take Sinjian with me. I could fill in the blank for her. Sinjian was under the table now, getting ready to escape. Lily didn't even notice.

"Didn't you know, Gracie?" she asked.

My face started to burn. "Sure. I knew," I said trying to make my voice sound normal. "I just . . . forgot."

Sinjian? Living with us? I couldn't believe it. Where was he going to sleep? We only have two bedrooms. I reached for a glass of water and noticed that my hand was trembling.

Lily relaxed in her chair and began chattering away.

"Well, I'm very glad the four of you will be moving to Salt Lake City. A boy like Sinjian will do better in an urban environment where there are more resources available to him. Small towns like this one cramp the soul. I know from personal experience," she laughed. "I grew up in one in Idaho."

"Salt Lake City!" Sarah exploded. She turned on me. "Why didn't you *tell* me you were moving to Salt Lake City, Gracie." She swore so loudly that the people sitting at the table next to us turned to stare again. One of them even said "shh!" to Sarah.

My face and my neck went hot, even my breasts against my slip. "But I didn't know!"

Lily looked from Sarah to me. "Damn," she said. "Me and my stupid mouth."

Shaking, I stood up. The blood rushed to my head and

for a minute the room went dark. I pushed away from the table and walked straight toward Mom and Pete.

"It's so nice of you to come," Mom was saying in her soft voice to an older couple.

"Why didn't you tell me we were moving to Salt Lake!" I said.

Mom's hand slipped like a fish from the palm of the man she was greeting. He and his wife stepped back, smiling nervously.

Mom turned her large eyes on me. "Oh, Baby—"

Pete turned to Mom. "You didn't tell her?" He was upset.

I thought Mom was going to cry.

Pete took a deep breath, then put his arms around Mom and me and said in a happy voice, "Don't worry you two. Everything is going to be just fine!"

I shook his arm off me and stared straight at Mom.

"We'll talk later, Gracie. Okay?" she said. Her brown eyes were begging me to go sit with Sarah again.

I could feel my chest heave up and down I was breathing so hard, but I didn't move. "No. I won't sit down."

Mom looked up at Pete and gave him a little smile. "Will you excuse us for a minute?"

"Of course! Sure! Anything for my favorite girls!" He laughed.

Mom and I went outside. She took a deep breath, reached out, and stroked the skin on my cheek.

I brushed her hand away.

"Don't be mad at me, Gracie," she said. "I was waiting for the best time to tell you—"

I laughed at her and she hung her head.

Good! I hope you feel awful.

"So when were you going to tell me about Sinjian?"

"Gracie, Gracie—"

I started pacing back and forth. "I *knew* you weren't telling me something! I knew it. I just knew it."

My fists were clenched into tight balls.

"I hate it when people lie."

"I didn't lie." Mom's voice trembled.

"Yes, you did! You let me think we were going to stay here in our own house. That's lying! You lied to me."

"Baby, I wanted to tell you that day at the mall—"

"This is my life, too, Mom! My life! I don't want to live in Salt Lake. I don't have any friends there. Please, Mom, please. We can't move! *Please—*"

If I said another word, just one more word, I would start crying.

Mom took a deep breath. "I already told you that Pete is quitting his job at Geneva so he can make a go of his Americalife business—"

I swore.

"—and he thinks he'll be more successful in Salt Lake City."

"You can't do this to me," I said. "You just—can't."

"We won't leave until school ends."

Nothing I said, nothing I did would change things.

There was a long silence between us. "I should have told you," said Mom. "That was very wrong of me."

A train whistled in the distance.

"Please," I whispered. "Please don't do this to me, Mama."

There were tears on her cheeks as she slipped her arm across my shoulder. I didn't shake it off.

"I'm sorry, Baby. I'm just so sorry." She lifted my hair so I could feel the cool April air on my neck.

"I hope you can forgive me," she said quietly.

I swallowed hard and nodded. Sure. Of course. Always.

But when I looked up at the stars I wished with all my heart that they would explode.

Explode and *burn* this night away.

chapter 6

"I can't believe I screamed at her in front of everybody," I said on the way home. "I feel like such an idiot."

"She deserved it. Salt Lake City." Sarah swore.

We were walking down the middle of the railroad tracks that run between the church and my house. Mrs. Macleod would have an absolute fit if she knew how often Sarah and I did this late at night—just walked along the tracks under a big bright moon and talked about things.

"I shouldn't have acted like that," I said. "She was still upset when she left."

After the reception Pete took Lily and Sinjian to a motel, then he and Mom left on their two-night honeymoon to Las Vegas in a car stuffed with crumpled newspapers and covered with balloons and shaving cream. People who do stuff like that, I've discovered, aren't usually the ones who have to clean it up afterward.

I sighed.

"I can't believe you're moving," Sarah said. "I hate people from Salt Lake."

"You don't know anybody from Salt Lake," I told her.

Sarah just shrugged and shoved her hands deep into the pockets of her leather jacket. "I see them at state football play-offs every year, don't I? They think they're so-o-o-o stinking special."

I remembered the time a group of us went to the girls' bathroom at halftime during a play-off game. Three Salt Lake girls standing by the sinks stopped talking when we walked in. Then one of them giggled and said loud enough for everybody to hear, "Hey you guys, look at the wuzzers."

Wuzzers. Because some people from American Fork like Mrs. Macleod say "we was" and "they was." I wanted to slap that girl's face.

We stepped off the tracks. "Hey! Nobody's going to be at your house tonight," Sarah said, "so why don't I sleep over? I love your house so much because nobody in my family lives there."

I laughed for the first time since Mom and Pete left.

"Can I sleep over, Gracie? Can I? Can I? Can I?" Sarah imitated her little brother Joshua.

"Not tonight, Sarah," I said finally. "Okay?" I wanted to be alone. I wanted time to think.

Sarah started to pout, then changed her mind. I guess she knew how I was feeling and figured she could spare me one of her bad moods. She began singing a song she'd heard on the radio instead. "I want to be your sweet-lovin' dum-dee-dum-dum-whatever-whatever . . ."

How many times had Sarah and I walked down this road during spring together? When we were little, Sarah used to say that the cherry blossoms smelled just like pig's feet, but I liked their thick scent.

I wouldn't be here next spring when the trees' rough dark branches turned white.

"Look," said Sarah when we finally got to my house, "you don't have to move to Salt Lake. You can stay here and live with me. What's one more body at my house?"

I fumbled for the key hidden under the doormat. "I don't think I ought to leave my mom right now."

Sarah sighed. "I *knew* you were going to say that."

I opened the front door and let myself in.

" 'Night, Sarah."

"I mean it, Gracie," she said, walking away. "You can come live with me whenever you want to."

The house was quiet except for the ticking of the mantel clock Mom got as a present for her *first* wedding. It was strange how such a little clock could make enough noise to fill the whole house. But then our house wasn't very big.

Some dirty dishes were in the kitchen sink. Pete, no doubt, just had to have himself a bowl of Frankenberry cereal before the reception and didn't bother to clean up after himself.

I jammed the stopper in the drain and turned the water on full blast so that it splashed all over my new dress.

I heard a sound in the backyard.

I turned the water off and listened.

There it was again!

I walked quietly out onto the back porch and looked around. A hungry yowl came from underneath the forsythia bush. The lower limbs rustled as a thin black cat emerged. It froze when it saw me.

I wanted to speak in a friendly low voice, tell it that everything was okay, but I knew if I said anything, it would disappear without eating the food I'd set out.

The cat watched me with gleaming eyes, then moved like a soldier on its belly carefully toward the food sitting about ten feet away from me. I barely breathed. When it reached the bowl, the cat crouched and ate fast. Every now and then it stopped and looked over its shoulder.

We had this ritual, the cat and I. I put food out. It came. But I knew that no matter how much I fed it, the cat would never come close enough for me to pet it. Maybe if it were still a kitten, things would be different. Maybe I could get it to trust me, but it was too late now. The cat had already gone wild.

This neighborhood is full of wild cats. People are always dropping off box loads of kittens in the fields around here. They tell themselves that some nice farmer will give them all a home in his barn, and then they drive away feeling pretty good about themselves. Well, I wish they would stick around long enough to see the kittens turn into cats with hollow ribs and running eyes.

This particular cat keeps coming back but I don't give

him a name because he doesn't belong to me or anybody else.

The cat finished its meal, threw me one last look, then darted away.

"Good-bye," I said to the air.

A mountain breeze blew suddenly through the yard, making me shiver. But I didn't go inside.

The tulip bulbs Mr. Messick helped me plant last fall were starting to bloom. He and I had big plans for our backyard. We were going to fill it with flowers—all kinds —but especially sunflowers. Sunflowers growing tall against the back fence. I love sunflowers best of all, their long heart-shaped leaves and their deep yellow petals and the way their rough brown faces follow the sun across the sky.

Silent tears slipped down my cheeks, making my collar wet. The wind died down and the night went perfectly quiet.

I was watching a rerun of *Magnum P.I.* when the doorbell rang. It was nearly eleven o'clock.

"Who is it?" I asked in a voice that sounded braver than I felt.

"It's Lily DuPre."

I opened the door. Sinjian was staring at his orange high-top shoes, but Lily gave me a friendly smile.

"Come in," I said.

"Hurry, Sinjian," she said. He walked through the door, dragging a suitcase behind him.

They sat down on the couch, and I took a seat across from them.

Lily looked around and whistled. "Boy, this place is really tidy. Pete must not be living here yet." She smiled at me again. "He's such a slob, don't you know. But then so am I. Some days things got so bad when we were together that everybody had to drink out of empty mason jars because all the cups were dirty." She laughed, then shrugged. "Oh well. Housekeeping never was one of my talents."

I've noticed that people who say that about themselves secretly believe their messiness is proof that they're really smarter and more creative than everybody else. They're just too busy doing important things to pick up after themselves.

"I like things to be neat," I said in a tight voice.

Lily narrowed her eyes a little as she studied my face. "I'm sure that's true. I can tell you're a *practical* person." She didn't make it sound like a compliment.

Lily draped an arm around Sinjian's shoulder. "Anyway, Gracie, I've come to ask you a very big favor. I was going to stay here in town tonight, but I've decided to drive on to Moab and stay with friends there. I've discussed this with Sinjian, and it's okay with him."

I looked at Sinjian who was sticking his chin out and banging his heels against the base of the couch.

"Can I leave him here with you tonight, Gracie?"

He was sitting on my couch in my house with a suitcase. What could I say?

58

"Yeah. You can stay here, Sinjian."

Lily clapped her hands together. "That's terrific!"

"Where's Moab?" Sinjian said.

"In southern Utah," said Lily. "In the desert."

"Why can't I go with you?"

Lily looked a little annoyed. "We already talked about it, Love. It wouldn't be fun for you. You'll have more fun with Gracie."

"Please, Mommy, *please*—"

"Sinjian!"

He slumped back in the couch.

Lily forced a smile. "I'll send you a present, okay? What do you want?"

Sinjian scrunched up his face while he thought. "A camel."

Lily looked confused.

"A camel?"

"So I can ride it to school. I want a camel from the desert."

Lily threw back her head and laughed hard. "Isn't he great?" she said to me. "Okay, Sinjian. If I find a camel, I'll send it to you."

"For reals?"

Lily nodded, then gave him a hug and kissed the top of his spikey hair. "Be a good boy. I love you."

We watched the last ten minutes of *Magnum* after Lily left, then I fixed Sinjian a bowl of cold cereal. Frankenberry.

"Isn't it getting kind of late for you?" I finally asked.

"Mom always lets me stay up as late as I want to. Sometimes I never go to bed." He was smacking his lips.

"Well, I'm going to bed now, and I think you should, too."

"Where's my bedroom?"

We had two bedrooms—one for Pete and Mom, the other for me. Where did they expect him to sleep?

"You can sleep in my mom's room tonight. She has a big soft bed. Sort of like the Mama Bear's bed in Goldilocks," I said as I picked up Sinjian's bowl and drained the pink milk down the sink.

Sinjian looked at me like he thought I was crazy.

"Come on," I said. "Let's go." Sinjian followed me into Mom's room.

"See?" I flipped on the lights. "This is a great bed. You'll love it."

He didn't move.

"Get ready for bed now," I said, trying to sound nice but strict.

Sinjian dropped his chin on his chest, then shuffled slowly across the floor. He crawled into Mom's bed with all of his clothes on, including shoes.

"Don't you have some pajamas?" I winced, thinking about those shoes against the clean sheets.

He blinked. "I like to sleep in my clothes. Then you don't have to get dressed in the morning."

I was speechless. What he said made sense in a strange sort of way.

"Okay fine," I grumbled. "But please take your shoes off."

Sinjian sat up, rolling his eyes like I'd asked him to clean the entire house by himself, and unlaced his high-tops. He pulled them off and let them drop to the floor.

I walked over to the side of the bed, bent over to pick up the shoes, then placed them side by side in the corner of the room. I turned to go. " 'Night, Sinjian."

"Leave the lights on," he said without saying please.

I went to my own room and plopped down on my bed.

Lying down made me realize how tired I was. I felt just like one of those cartoon characters that gets flattened by a steam roller. I wanted to sleep for days and weeks, only my mind was still racing.

What was I going to do with this weird little kid sleeping in Mom's bed?

The moon was shining through my window. A couple of nights ago it had been bright and round, but now it was fading away.

I had a kaleidoscope once.

I got it at my birthday party when I turned seven. At first I didn't even know what it was. I took it out of the box and turned it over in my hands, trying to figure it out.

"It's one of them things pirates use," somebody said.

Mom laughed. "No, it's a kaleidoscope. Give it to me, Baby, and I'll show you kids how it works."

I handed it to her. "Okay," she said, "this is what you do. Put the small end up to your eye like this. See? Then close your other eye like you're winking at all your boyfriends . . ." Everybody giggled. "Now point it toward a window so that you get the light, then twist the ring on the big end just like this." She paused. "Look, Gracie!"

She held the kaleidoscope to my eye and I looked. The bits of colored glass had settled into a pattern that looked like butterfly wings.

"Hey, I want to see!" One of the kids grabbed the kaleidoscope out of Mom's hands.

"I wasn't finished!" I yelled, but Mom said, "Gracie, you need to share," so everybody took a turn looking through the kaleidoscope. By the time it got back to me, the butterfly wings were gone, and no matter how many times I twisted the knob, I couldn't get them back.

The same thing was happening to me right now.

I heard a rustling noise in the hallway, then Sinjian poked his head through my door.

"How come you're out of bed?" I asked.

He stepped all the way into my room, then glanced nervously over his shoulder. Even though it was dark, I could see the whites of his eyes glowing.

"I think maybe there are some ghoulies in that room." He whispered the word *ghoulies.*

"Don't be silly," I said. "There aren't any such things as ghoulies."

"Yes there are. My baby-sitter and I saw a movie about them. They live in people's toilets."

Can you believe it, some stupid baby-sitter letting a kid watch a movie like that?

"That was just pretend, Sinjian. Special effects."

He didn't budge.

"I promise . . ."

He still didn't move.

"Can I sleep with you, Gracie?"

Now I swallowed. "Well, this isn't a very big bed."

"I could sleep on the floor. I love sleeping on the floor."

I sighed. "Okay. Fine. Just for tonight."

"Yes!" Sinjian screamed like he'd just scored the winning basket.

"Go get a pillow off Mom's bed," I said.

"I can't because of—you know"—his voice dropped—"the ghoulies."

I stomped out of my room and returned with a pillow. Sinjian didn't say thanks. I crawled back into my bed and turned my face to the wall when it struck me: after all these years alone I was sharing a room with a kid, just like Sarah. I didn't know whether to laugh or cry.

"Anyways"—Sinjian's voice came floating up from the floor—"do you know how I know karate? Because I was born in China. For reals."

SALT LAKE CITY, JULY

chapter 7

~~~~~~~~~~~~~~~~~~~ ◆

It was 105 degrees the day we rolled into Salt Lake City—a new record for July, the radio said.

Mom, Pete, Sinjian, and I were crowded into the cab of Pete's old pickup, sweating like crazy in spite of the blasts of hot air shooting through the open windows. The bed of the truck was loaded with boxes, furniture, and mattresses that Pete had tried to protect with a tarp. One of the straps, however, came loose somewhere between American Fork and Salt Lake, so that the sheet of black plastic whipped and flapped around like some giant bat.

I felt just like the Okie family in that old Henry Fonda movie we saw in English class—*The Grapes of Wrath*.

The only good thing I could see about moving to Salt Lake City was that I'd have a room to myself.

Pete *promised*.

I asked him about it as soon as he and Mom got back

67

from their honeymoon. After spending the weekend alone with Sinjian, I knew I had to have my own room.

Sinjian had followed me everywhere. I was afraid he'd even crawl into the bathtub with me, so I locked the door.

He waited for me in the hall.

Finally, after I couldn't take it anymore, I told him we were going to Sarah's house. "She has lots of brothers and sisters you can play with."

"What are their names?" Sinjian asked.

I told him.

"Well, I don't think I know any of them," he said.

"You'll have fun. I promise."

Sinjian dragged behind me on the way to Sarah's, picking up rocks and stuffing them into his pockets so that the sides of his pants bulged.

"For my rock collection," he explained.

Mrs. Macleod took Sinjian by the hand when we arrived and led him downstairs where Rachel and Rebecca were playing. But in five minutes he was at my side again, hanging out in the kitchen with Sarah and me.

"They were playing Barbies," he said. "Barbies suck."

"You guys want something to drink?" Sarah asked, going to the fridge. "We have root beer left over from Danny's birthday party."

"You know how they made root beer in the olden days?" Sinjian said. "Out of beer and roots."

Sarah laughed and I smiled.

"It's true, you guys!"

"I don't think so," I said.

Sinjian folded his arms and pouted while Sarah mouthed the words "This kid is weird."

I shrugged like I didn't know what I was going to do about it. I looked at him, though, his hands and face all dirty from gathering rocks, and I felt a little tug inside.

Later that night I found piles of gravel and grit on my bed.

Sinjian had emptied his pockets there!

"Sinjian!" I marched into the living room where he was watching TV while eating a bowl of cereal. "There are rocks all over my bed."

He looked up at me and blinked. "Well, I didn't put them there."

I thought of the white bedspread, now gray with dirt.

"Don't lie to me!" I snapped.

Sinjian's eyes widened. Then he scampered from the room and slammed my door behind him. Taking a deep breath, I followed him.

He was sitting with his rocks in the middle of my bed, crying. "Geez! Everybody's always screaming at me!"

"I'm sorry," I said. "Please stop crying."

He snuffled a little while wiping his eyes with the back of his hand.

"Let's pick these up together. Okay?" I said.

He reached for a rock and stuffed it back into his pocket.

"There's a place in France," he sang, "where the ladies wear no pants . . ."

No doubt about it. I *had* to have my own room.

69

"We're almost there. This is the Avenues," Pete said as he turned up from South Temple Street onto a narrow tree-lined road. "It's one of the original old neighborhoods in Salt Lake. We're gonna love it!"

I looked at Mom. She was wearing the same old clothes she'd worn yesterday and the day before that when we were packing to leave. The pink top was dirty and the pants were starting to bag around her waist. She gave me a tired smile and reached for my hand.

The houses stood close together—big ones next to small ones, wood houses next to brick. Most of them were old. Victorian. Some of them had been fixed up to look like the painted houses you see in books about San Francisco. Others were run-down, with trash collecting on the porches and dry weeds waving in the small yards. Pete had said we were going to be living in a duplex.

"Ah! Here we go!" Pete turned down a narrow one-way street that was filled with police cars and two trucks that said Division of Wildlife Services.

"What's—what's going on here?" Mom asked. They were practically the first words she'd said since leaving American Fork.

Sinjian bounced around on the seat.

Pete pulled over.

A couple of cops were escorting a man out of an orange brick house. He was wearing a cowboy hat, an old pair of faded bell-bottoms, and a leather vest without a shirt.

"Hey! You are violating my religious rights!" the man yelled. "I'm calling the ACLU!"

"You do that," said one of the cops.

They were followed by a man carrying a golden eagle and a couple of magpies that had been stuffed. "Look what I found," he called to the cops.

"I have Indian blood! Those birds are a part of my religion!"

"Right," said the other cop.

There was a crowd of people watching—an old lady with a walker, a little girl, a guy with a ponytail on a mountain bike, a young mother with a baby, two boys my age with skateboards tucked under their arms, a man in a gray suit. Most of them were smiling.

Pete called to the biker. "What's going on here?"

The guy laughed. "That's Jesse. As in James. God only knows what his real name is. He builds a bonfire in his backyard on weekends and chants. I guess he finally gave the police a good enough excuse to go through his place. Looks like he's got himself a collection of endangered species."

"Is—is he dangerous?" Pete asked.

"Naw. Just a little local color." He pushed off on his bike and was gone.

"The man in the cowboy hat," said Sinjian, "he looks kind of mean."

"Don't worry about him," Pete said, although he sounded worried himself. "He's just a few fries short of a

Happy Meal." He laughed. "Get it, Sinjian? A few fries short?"

"I don't think I really want to live here," said Sinjian, sinking into the seat.

I didn't either.

"Don't whine!" Pete snapped. "See? There's the place right up there." He pointed at a very small single story red-brick house with two front doors and two front porches. There was a cat tied up with a piece of string on one of them. "It's little, but it will do for now until we get on our feet." He looked at Mom, suddenly worried. "What do you think, Cynthia?"

"I think it's great," she said without really looking. She gave Pete a weak smile.

"I *said* I don't want to live here," said Sinjian.

Pete turned on Sinjian. "And I said *don't whine!*"

Welcome to Salt Lake City.

The inside of the duplex was clean, empty, and small with beige walls, beige blinds, and beige tile floors.

I raced through the house to check things out. Sinjian trailed me like a puppy from the living room to the kitchen to the bathroom to the two bedrooms.

Two bedrooms.

I stomped into the living room where Mom stood looking around and folding her arms.

"I thought I was going to have my own bedroom."

"What?" Mom looked surprised to see me standing at her side.

I tapped my foot. "You should have helped him pick out a place, Mom."

"I'm sorry," she said.

I let out a deep breath, counted to ten in my head, did all the things people tell you to do so you won't get mad. Finally, I spun around and went outside. Pete was grunting as he walked up the steps with a couple of Americalife boxes.

"I don't want to share a room with Sinjian anymore," I said. "You said when we moved to Salt Lake I wouldn't have to share a room with him."

Sweat rolled off the end of Pete's nose. "Can we please talk about this later?"

"I'm almost sixteen," I said. "I shouldn't have to share a room with a little boy!"

Pete put down the boxes and wiped his forehead. "It sure is hot today. The weatherman said it was supposed to rain."

"Weathermen are idiots," I said. "I want my own room."

Pete looked me straight in the eyes. "This is the best I could do for now, Gracie. It's only for six months. When the lease runs out we'll have enough money to buy the kind of place we want. You'll have your own room then."

Sinjian burst through the front door. "Come look, Gracie! I want to show you something!"

I glared at Pete, then followed Sinjian inside. He led me to one of the bedrooms.

"This one's ours," he said. "Look! It has shelves already built on the wall. Can I keep my collections there?"

Sinjian collects everything—rocks, junky toys out of gumball machines, candy wrappers. He even has a stack of clothing labels, the kind that say WASH IN WARM WATER/ TUMBLE LOW that he cut out from the necks of his T-shirts. He spread his collections all over my room at the old house, which made me crazy.

"If you promise to keep all your stuff on those shelves you can have them," I said. "And now I want to show *you* something." I stomped in a straight line down the middle of the room. "Pretend there is a fence right here where I'm walking. You keep your things on your side of the room. I'll keep my things on my side. Okay?"

He nodded.

"I mean it, Sinjian. You can't leave your stuff all around like you did in American Fork. It isn't fair."

"Cross my heart and hope to die. Stick a needle in your eye."

"*Your* eye," I said. "Not my eye. You don't stick the needle in my eye."

Sinjian gave me a strange look, and I realized how stupid I was sounding.

"Sinjian! Gracie! I need you guys to help me haul this stuff from the truck in here," Pete called.

When I walked through the empty living room, I saw Mom staring out the window. Not looking at anything. Just staring.

*   *   *

74

Pete decided to get his Americalife business going that same day. "There's no time like the present!" he said.

Sinjian and I distributed fliers around the neighborhood inviting people to COME FIND OUT HOW YOU CAN LOSE WEIGHT—AND MAKE MONEY, TOO!

When Thursday came our duplex was still filled with unpacked boxes. I couldn't stand looking around the room at all those sagging cardboard boxes stacked on top of each other. I was going through them, one by one, trying to find places for everybody's things. Pete's boxes were the worst. He had a million of them, filled with junk he's spent his whole life collecting—old sneakers, magazines, matchbooks, pennies—things he'll never use in a million years.

"What am I supposed to do with this?" I'd ask, holding up something.

"Don't worry about it," he'd say. "I'll take care of it."

But he never did.

I found his old high school yearbook and stopped unpacking long enough to look through it. The class pictures were pretty funny. The guys had long sideburns and shaggy hair, and the girls all parted their long hair down the middle so they looked just like Cher when she was still with Sonny. I laughed until I saw Mom's picture. Smiling straight into the camera, she looked as normal and happy as the next girl. Except for the hair, she looked just like me. I snapped the book shut and buried it deep in the box.

"Are you still planning on having your stupid Americalife meeting here tonight?" I asked. My heart was beating a little faster, getting ready for a fight.

"Where am I supposed to have my meeting, Gracie?" Pete was trying to be patient.

"Pete! We can't have people here. Look around you!"

Pete looked around him. "No one will mind," he said weakly. "They probably won't even notice—"

"You don't think anybody's going to notice a room full of unpacked boxes?"

"Now don't you go yelling at me!" Pete snapped. He glanced toward his bedroom where Mom was lying on a mattress with no sheets, then lowered his voice. "I told you I don't want anybody to wake up Cynthia. She doesn't feel good."

I wasn't feeling so hot myself. It makes me crazy the way Pete never thinks things through.

Just then I heard Sinjian crying on the front porch. Pete's lips went tight.

Sinjian rang the doorbell, screaming bloody murder. You know how you can tell from a kid's cry whether he's really hurt or not? Sinjian was just crying to get attention. He does it all the time.

"The door's open," I called.

He cried louder and rang the doorbell.

"Come on in, Sinjian," Pete said, trying to be patient. *Briing! Briing!*

I marched over and opened the door.

"What's the matter?" Pete asked.

Sinjian plopped down in the middle of the floor and folded his arms across his chest. He started pouting.

"I can't help you if you don't tell me what the matter is," said Pete, his voice getting louder. Sinjian just sat there.

Pete heaved a big sigh. "I do *not* have time for this." He got up and shuffled toward the bedroom where Mom was resting.

"Seven o'clock tonight, Gracie," he called to me before shutting the door. "That's what time the meeting is. If your mother isn't feeling better, I'll need your help."

"I'm hungry," Sinjian whined.

"Fine. Okay. Come help me fix you something to eat."

Sinjian followed me into the kitchen, then sat down and watched while I started pulling things out of the cupboard to make the peanut butter sandwiches.

"So what's the matter?" I asked.

He threw out his chin like he wasn't going to talk no matter what I did to him.

"Fine," I said. "Don't tell me then."

"Some big kids up the street. They told me they were going to beat me up."

I finished spreading the peanut butter and started spreading the jam. Frozen raspberry. I made it last summer. "Why are they going to beat you up?" I figured Sinjian probably did something that made them want to beat him up. I often feel like doing it myself.

"Because they hate me. Everybody hates me."

I sighed. You have to take a million little verbal detours

77

in a conversation with Sinjian. "Everybody does not hate you. I promise. Did you do something to make these big kids mad?"

He shrugged as he took the sandwich I handed him. "I just told them I was a real-life ninja and that I knew how to make them all blind in one of their eyes. So then they told me they were going to kill me."

"How old are these guys?"

"Nine or ten, I guess," he said, his mouth full of peanut butter. "They were pretty big, too. Giants."

I just stared at him. "Sinjian," I said finally, "don't go around telling people you know how to poke their eyes out, especially if they're bigger and older than you are."

"But it's true," he said.

"What's true," I said. "That you know how to make people blind?"

"No—that I'm a real-life ninja."

I heard a noise coming from the bedroom. It sounded like someone was crying. My mother. When she wasn't sleeping these days, she was crying. She'd been this way ever since we'd moved.

"What's the matter, Cynthia?" Pete said.

I felt the palms of my hands go moist.

"You can watch TV after you eat," I told Sinjian in an unsteady voice. "I'm going for a walk."

"I want to come with you," he said.

"No!"

Sinjian started to pout, but I ignored him. I put away the peanut butter and jam, and I ran out the front door.

It was warm outside, warmer than it ever feels at home even though American Fork is maybe only thirty miles away from Salt Lake. It was all the asphalt, trapping the sun's dry white rays

I walked fast—as though my feet were trying to catch up with the thoughts racing through my head.

Mom was getting sick again. I couldn't pretend it wasn't happening anymore because all the signs were there. She wasn't eating and she wasn't sleeping at night. She wasn't combing her hair or getting dressed in the morning or talking much unless people talked to her first. She was turning back into a shadow.

Think, Gracie, think.

Little beads of sweat gathered on my forehead. The sound of my own footsteps filled my ears.

Think. What happened this time? What started her off? What did you do?

Think!

chapter 8

Mom was sleeping and Pete was out running errands when I got back from my walk.

I made Sinjian help me unpack a few more boxes, and then we stashed the rest under the table and in the corners. I dusted and put my plants in the windowsills and tried to arrange the furniture so that people would at least have a place to sit down. After I got the living room organized, I started to make cookies for refreshments. One thing I have to say about myself is that I do make pretty good cookies. I make all kinds—oatmeal, lemon bars, Mexican wedding cookies, shortbread, sugar cookies filled with raisins or fresh raspberry jam, cream cheese cookies. My favorite cookie, however, is still plain old chocolate chip, only I always add more salt than most people do. The tastes of chocolate and salt are good with each other.

"What about flowers?" Sinjian asked.

"What?"

"Flowers. You know. For decorations."

I paused. Flowers would be very nice.

"Fine," I said. "You take care of the flowers." Anything to get him out of my hair.

Sinjian ran out the screen door and let it bang, which always makes Pete jump straight out of his skin.

Pete came in about five minutes later and walked through without noticing how clean the house was.

After checking on Mom, Pete came into the kitchen where he reached over my shoulder to help himself to a big glob of cookie dough. I pulled away when his skin touched mine.

"I guess you better plan on helping me out tonight," he said with a full mouth.

I wanted to yell. *What do you think I've been doing all afternoon!*

The doorbell rang.

"Get that, okay?" Pete was too busy eating dough.

As I walked into the living room, I saw a boy about my age through the screen door. He was just looking around, wearing shorts, a baseball cap, and a cutaway T-shirt that said NIKE. He had a skateboard tucked underneath one arm.

"Can I help you?"

His eyes were light green—almost the color of aspen leaves. He wasn't that tall, but he was very nice-looking: blond hair, sun-brown skin, strong shoulders. Also, he had a little gold stud in one ear. I know lots of guys have their ears pierced, but I always think it looks a little strange at first.

He reached into his back pocket and pulled out one of Pete's fliers about tonight's Americalife meeting. It was all wadded up.

"I wanted to talk to somebody about this. Can I come in?" he asked, without smiling.

I opened the screen door. When I'm nervous I can't think of a single thing to say.

He came inside and sat down.

"I just wanted to find out more about this deal you're having here tonight." He didn't look happy.

"Well," I said, sitting down on a sofa across from him, "it's my stepfather's business. Americalife is a line of health-type products."

Did he notice that my jeans were dirty? That my hair wasn't washed yet?

"But it says here that other people can make a lot of money, too."

"You can if you want to sell Americalife. You buy a distributor's kit from my stepdad and start your own business." I felt my face go red. This kid probably thought I was trying to sell him on Americalife. But I found myself saying the same words Pete always says because I couldn't think of any of my own.

"Oh right," he said, really angry now. "Then I sign up ten more people who sign up ten more people who sign up ten more people and we all get a cut of the sales other people make." He snorted. "It's nothing but a stupid pyramid scheme."

"It's not a pyramid scheme!"

We turned around and looked at Pete in the kitchen door, shouting at us. I couldn't believe it.

"Okay," said the boy calmly, "then what do you call it?"

"I call it multilevel marketing," said Pete. He was speaking in a normal voice now, but I wanted to slip like loose change through the cushions of the sofa. Pete was smiling and moving toward us. "Sorry I lost my temper, but the words 'pyramid scheme' have a real negative connotation to me. My name is Peter Wilding and this is my daughter, Gracie." My daughter? I winced as Pete shook hands with the boy.

"My name is Tiimo Lehtinen," he said.

"Tiimo," said Pete. "What kind of a name is that?"

"Finnish. I was born in Finland."

"Finland," said Pete. "Now there's one place I've never been."

I couldn't believe how Pete was talking like some big world traveler when in fact he's never been anywhere.

"Anyway," said Tiimo, stuffing the flier back into his pocket, "I think I found out what this is about."

"Good!" said Pete. "Great. Come back tonight and learn more about the Americalife opportunity!"

"I'm sure I'll be back," said Tiimo, only he didn't sound too thrilled about it. Then he left. Nobody said good-bye.

I watched him walk down the stairs, get on his

skateboard, and push himself up the street. Where did he live? I'd probably never find out. He'd avoid me forever and tell all his friends how stupid we were with our Americalife pills and powders.

I turned to Pete.

"Oh this is great—just great!" I said. All of a sudden I felt like crying, which made me even madder.

His mouth popped open. "What are you complaining about? He said he'd be coming back."

My face started to burn.

Just then Sinjian slipped through the front door, smiling and carrying some potted mums in both hands. They looked like they cost money.

"Where did you get those?" I snapped.

Pete stopped telling me that Tiimo was coming back and stared at Sinjian, too. Sinjian looked at me, then at Pete, then back at me again. The smile slipped right off his face.

Whenever Sinjian gets ready to lie (which is almost all the time) his eyes widen. Then he licks his lips and starts jiggling around, shifting his weight from foot to foot.

"I got them from a lady who lives up the street," he said, swaying back and forth. "She just gave them to me because she said she didn't want them anymore."

"Sin-jian!" The tone of my voice said I didn't believe him. Meanwhile his eyes were getting as big as silver dollars.

"It's true—"

"Did you steal those flowers?" Pete asked. "Well? Did you?"

Sinjian's face started to turn red. He looked mad and miserable all at once. Pete moved toward him saying, "I mean it. Don't lie to me."

I was sorry I even brought the whole thing up. "It doesn't matter."

"It does too matter," said Pete. "I don't want a thief for a son."

A thief. Sinjian takes a few flowers and this makes him an instant thief, which is just the kind of thing Pete says all the time. Sinjian started to cry. He shoved the pot of mums into my hands and said, "I don't care what you guys think. I don't care!" He ran out of the room still screaming *I-don't-care, I-don't-care.*

Pete and I looked at each other, then he plopped into a nearby chair and stared at a wall. I put the flowers in the middle of the dining room table and sat down myself. My arms and legs felt limp.

I looked at Sinjian's flowers. They were purple with bright yellow centers. I reached out to touch one of them. The yellow felt fuzzy—like a bee without a stinger. The petals felt like cool skin. Sinjian's flowers—wherever they came from—were very beautiful.

Tiimo came to the meeting that night with his mother and his grandmother. Tiimo's mother Ulla was in her early forties, tan and trim without being really thin, which I liked. She had short blond hair the color of Tiimo's, and her eyes were green like his, too. She wore running shoes, jeans, and a T-shirt that said SALT LAKE CITY CLASSIC 10K. She smiled a lot but I could tell she was shy. It always surprises me when I realize someone my mom's age is shy. You'd think they would have grown out of it.

Tiimo's grandmother was short and plump—a little like the fairy godmother in the movie *Cinderella*. I almost thought she'd take out a wand and sing "Bippity-boppity-boo!"

Maybe she could make me disappear.

As it was I was sitting in the front so I could hold up Pete's Americalife visual aids. Counting Tiimo and his family there were eight people—a young married couple with a baby, a tall thin guy with slicked-back hair and an Adam's apple that looked like a granny knot, a middle-aged woman. Pete went around the room introducing himself and shaking everybody's hand. You could see big half-moons of perspiration under the arms of his shirt he was already sweating so hard. I looked the other way.

"Well," said Pete when he got back to the front of the room, "it looks like it's about time to start. I want to thank you all for coming tonight—"

Just then, Mom walked into the room and sat down next to me. Her hair was combed, and she had lipstick on. She looked better than she'd looked for days.

Pete was surprised and pleased. "Folks"—I cringed at such a jolly *fake* word—"I want you all to meet my beautiful wife, Cynthia."

Mom turned and smiled brightly at everyone.

86

"Well now," Pete started, "I want to ask you all a question. What would *you* do if you had one thousand extra dollars a month?"

He looked around the room. No one raised a hand.

Pete gave a nervous little laugh. "Come on now. Don't be bashful."

Bashful? Bored is more like it.

Finally the woman with the baby raised her hand. You could tell she'd probably been the kind of kid who answered questions in school just to help the teacher out because nobody else would cooperate. The kind of kid that Sarah hated.

What would Sarah do if Pete asked her to help at an Americalife meeting? Blow smoke in his face?

"Yes," said Pete, looking relieved. "Please share your dream with us."

"Well, I don't know if this is my dream or anything, but I'd probably pay down on my Visa." Her baby started to cry. She popped a pacifier in his mouth like a plug. Everybody laughed a little.

"Good answer!" said Pete, just like she was a contestant on *Family Feud.* "Who else will share their dreams with us?"

Everytime Pete said the word "dreams" I shriveled up inside.

"Don't be shy. We're all friends here."

No one answered. Pete started to pace a little in front of the group. Every now and then he wiped the palms of his hands on his pants. "How would you like to make one thousand, five thousand, even ten thousand dollars a month?"

I just happened to see Tiimo's face at that moment. He rolled his eyes and folded his arms across his chest, then leaned back in his chair and stared at Pete like he wished Pete would drop dead.

I looked away fast. The room felt hot and stuffy, and I had a hard time breathing.

"Well, let me tell you about the Americalife opportunity," said Pete. Pete nodded at me. That was my cue to stand up in front of the group and display a poster featuring Americalife products. The poster said "Leap into Americalife . . . Today!" I held it in front of my face.

"Now," said Pete, "you can make a handsome income for yourself just by selling Americalife health products to friends and associates. But the really big money comes if you can sponsor those same people in your own Americalife business. Teach them how they can become distributors, too. Bring them into your network and show them how to bring other people into your network, too. You'll enjoy a share in the profits of everyone downline from you."

I put down the poster of Americalife products and held up a large flow sheet showing how the Americalife network-marketing concept works. Pete began explaining.

I shut out the drone of his voice and tried very hard to stare straight ahead. I felt Tiimo looking at me. I ignored his stare for a minute or two, but then I looked straight back at him. We stared at each other like that until he finally turned his head.

Pete's presentation went on for another twenty minutes that felt like twenty hours. Mom sat perfectly still in her chair the whole time, a faraway look in her eyes. After he was finished, people came up to talk to him and look at the sample products. Most of them were just being polite.

Tiimo hung behind while his mother and grandmother talked to Pete. Actually, Tiimo's mother did all the talking. I had the feeling that his grandmother didn't speak English.

"I'm very interested," Ulla said. "I would just like a little more time to think, you know?" I loved her accent. Tiimo didn't have an accent at all. Maybe he didn't even speak Finnish anymore.

"Let's go, Mom," I heard him mumble. "Please."

Ulla said something to Tiimo's grandmother who bobbed her head up and down.

Ulla smiled at Pete and me—a nice smile. "Thank you very much," she said.

"*Kiitos,*" said the grandmother with a little nod. Then she and Ulla walked toward the front door. Tiimo followed.

"Hey, if you have any questions . . ." Pete called after them. He waved.

One by one the people left. Sinjian came out of our room and grabbed a handful of cookies. Mom sat down on the couch and stared out the window.

"Thanks for being here, Cynthia," he said.

She looked up at him, surprised to hear her name.

I snorted. Why did it always happen this way? When other people were around—she talked, laughed, acted normal. But the *minute* they left, she turned into a zombie.

"How do you think it went?" Pete asked.

"I think it went fine," Mom said. She smiled but her eyes were blank.

"Some of them were definitely interested. Gracie's boyfriend with the earring—his mother was, for instance."

I clenched my teeth. "He *isn't* my boyfriend."

"Well, ex-c-u-u-u-u-s-e me!" Pete was trying to be funny.

I couldn't stand it for another minute. "I'll clean up this mess tomorrow—that is unless you guys want to clean it up tonight."

Mom and Pete both looked at me like I was speaking in tongues.

"I'm going to my room."

Once I was inside my *half* of the room I lay down on my bed and stared at the blank walls. I hadn't had time to put up my own posters and photographs.

A car, its radio blaring, gunned down the street. Somewhere a lady laughed. A baby cried.

I rolled over and reached for the radio on my nightstand. I turned the tuning knob slowly, picking up different stations as I did.

"—a nice number by Hank Williams, Jr.—crackle,

crackle—we are saved through the grace of our savior the Lord Jesus—crackle—*Oye' muchachos*—"

The voices filled my dark room, making me feel like I was connected to other people, even if it was only other people like me, out there listening to their radios alone at night.

"—some classic Stones on Z93!—"

I buried my face in a cool pillow.

Sarah, Sarah. I miss you.

The bedroom door opened. Sinjian slipped through the crack as quick as light and shut the door behind him. He hardly made a noise.

I didn't say anything to him, just listened to him take off his shoes and crawl into bed. Without even looking at him, I knew he still had on all his clothes, including his glove.

"—some people think Ravel meant this piece as a critique of the corrupt society that was eventually cleansed by the war—crackle—"

"Gracie," Sinjian whispered. "Know where I got those flowers from?"

I shook my head.

"Well, you know that old cemetery?"

The Salt Lake City Cemetery, where they buried every famous dead Mormon pioneer you ever heard of, is at the end of our street. Trust Pete to move us right next door to a graveyard.

"Sure," I mumbled.

"That's where I got the flowers from. I just saw them sitting there on top of a grave. I didn't think anybody would care if I took them. Honest, Gracie," he said. "Honest . . ."

chapter 9

～～～～～～ ◆

The next morning when I looked into the mirror I hated my dark eyes and hair. I wanted hair the color of sun. Sarah once tried to talk me into bleaching my hair the way she does, and I almost did, but finally I was afraid that it would look too fake.

I sighed. Some new makeup would definitely help. I had a little money —maybe even enough for the kind of makeup you buy at a nice department store like Nordstrom instead of the cheap kind I always buy at Smith's Food King.

I combed my hair, grabbed my purse, and walked out the front door. I planned to catch a bus on South Temple Street that would take me downtown.

One thing about living in the city is that there are lots of places to go and be with people if you don't have any friends.

"Gracie! Gracie!" Sinjian screamed at me as soon as I stepped outside. "Tatiana's loose again."

Tatiana is the cat who belongs to Mrs. Burns, the woman who lives in the other side of our duplex.

Tatiana's white fur is so long she probably collects dust when she walks across a room. She even looks like a mop. Four times a day, Mrs. Burns brings her outside and ties her up on the porch with a little piece of string for exactly one hour.

"You just can't let a valuable animal like this roam," Mrs. Burns always yells over to Pete if he happens to be outside when she ties up Tatiana. "No telling who might steal her. There are gangs of cat thieves in this city, yessiree, just waiting to turn cats like Tatiana into fur coats." Then she makes little kissing noises at Tatiana and goes inside.

Tying up a cat seemed about as wrong to me as abandoning one. I guess it has never occurred to Mrs. Burns that a cat who's tied up is a lot easier to steal than a cat who isn't—especially at night. She just didn't think. This made me *crazy.*

Meanwhile, Tatiana is always getting loose.

"I'm going to catch her for Mrs. Burns," Sinjian was saying. "Do you want to help me?"

"Not right now. I'm going downtown."

I started to walk down the front stairs when Mrs. Burns came barreling out of her front door, nearly knocking me over.

"You!" she screamed at Sinjian. "What did you do to my cat?"

94

Sinjian stopped dead in his tracks, then darted behind one of the box elder trees that line the street.

Mrs. Burns streaked after him, her house slippers slapping the soles of her feet. "You come back here!" she screeched. "Come back here right now!"

My face went hot.

"Mrs. Burns!" I went after her. When I caught her, I grabbed her by the upper arm. It felt flabby and cold as a fish in my hand. Mrs. Burns pulled her arm away and glared at me. For a minute I thought she might spit in my face. "Mrs. Burns," I said, trying to catch my breath, "Sinjian was only trying to catch Tatiana. She got loose again."

She snorted like she thought I was lying.

The blood rushed to my head. I was shaking. "Anyway," I said, my voice trembling, "it's really stupid to tie up a cat like that. What if a dog took after her? Tatiana would be a sitting duck. Didn't you ever think about that?"

Mrs. Burns mouth fell open like the slot on a gumball machine.

"Sinjian!" I yelled. He stepped out from behind his tree. "Come on. You're going downtown with me."

He stood there in shock. I was actually offering to take him someplace with me.

"Hurry up!"

Sinjian started to cry, then ran straight to me. I grabbed his sticky hand hard, and we started walking down the street. Fast.

"If I ever catch either one of you bothering Tatiana again . . ." Mrs. Burns was screaming after us.

"Just ignore her," I said. Sinjian was still crying.

He kept it up, too—huge choking sobs—all the way to the bus stop. There were two people waiting, a girl with a backpack who was probably a student at the University of Utah and a very old lady wearing a hat and gloves. They both stared at us.

"Hush," I whispered. "Please!"

"Geez! Geez! I was just trying to help." He cried some more.

"If you don't stop crying right now," I whispered loudly, "I won't let you go with me. I mean it."

I couldn't believe it. Sinjian actually stopped crying, and the student and the old lady in the hat stopped looking at us. The bus rolled up. I paid our fare, and Sinjian and I took the bench seat at the very back.

"I like to sit in the back," said Sinjian. "Don't you?" He started bouncing up and down on the blue vinyl cushion.

"I never thought about it," I said, turning to look out the window.

Up and down, up and down, up and down.

"Gracie, did you know there was a dinosaur that was as big as five Empire State Buildings?" Sinjian is the world's foremost authority on dinosaurs.

"Sin-jian."

"For reals. I promise."

I looked him straight in the eye. "Stop saying stuff that

96

isn't true. It gets you into trouble. There never was a dinosaur as big as five Empire State Buildings."

He thought. "Oh yeah, I forgot. I meant to say that there was a dinosaur that could eat trees as big as five Empire State Buildings."

You can never win an argument with Sinjian. I looked back out the window as he bounced up and down, up and down.

Sinjian. Talk about your goofy names. Where did Lily get a name like that? Maybe she used to watch a lot of daytime television. Guys on the soaps always have such strange names—Buzz, Cruz, Dakota. Names you never hear in real life. Or maybe she knew someone named Sinjian in one of her previous lives.

The bus rumbled down South Temple, which is one of the main streets in Salt Lake City. You can tell that old stone and brick mansions with fairy-tale towers once lined the entire street. I closed my eyes for a second and imagined myself getting out of a horse-drawn carriage in front of one of them. The picture made me smile.

Some of the old houses are gone now, replaced with apartment and office buildings, but the street is still very beautiful, and you can believe by just looking at it that people with a lot of money still live in the city.

Sinjian started to sing. "Jingle bells, Batman smells, Robin laid an egg—"

"Shh!"

"—the batmobile broke a wheel, and the Joker ran away!"

97

I couldn't help it. I started to laugh. "Where do you get these songs?"

"Nowhere," said Sinjian. "I just—you know—invent them."

I shook my head, but I was still smiling when I looked out the window.

We got off the bus in front of the Crossroads Mall downtown. Yellow banners with appliquéd covered wagons and the words DAYS OF '47 waved from street lamps up and down Main. Soon it would be the 24th of July, which is the day everybody in Utah celebrates the entry of the Mormon pioneers into the Salt Lake Valley. Maybe Sarah would come up to go to the big rodeo in the Salt Palace. Sarah loves rodeos.

"Can we go to Busy Bee Toy Store? It's in the mall," Sinjian said. "Ple-a-a-s-e!"

What could I say?

"We'll go after I do what I want to do, but only if you stop whining. And you can't ask for anything there either. Okay?"

As it turned out, I didn't much feel like looking at makeup. Sinjian kept opening up tubes of sample lipstick and swiveling them as high as they would go.

"Hey, look at *this* color," he'd say so that everybody could hear. "Awesome, huh?"

"Okay, Sinjian," I finally said. "Let's go to Busy Bee."

Sinjian ran straight to the back of the store to look at GI Joes while I stayed in the front and waited for him.

Since I didn't have anything better to do, I looked at the dolls in the doll case.

That's when I saw *her* for the first time.

Along with the usual Cabbage Patch and Madame Alexanders, there was the most beautiful doll I had ever seen. She was porcelain, with creamy white skin and long dark curls—just the kind of hair I wanted when I was little. Her eyes were blue with thick lashes, and her mouth and cheeks were dark pink. She was wearing an old-fashioned velvet cape trimmed with fur and a big fur hat. A little muff perched on one hand, and a pair of tiny skates dangled from the other.

Amelia. If she were mine, I'd call her Amelia.

"How much is that doll?" I asked suddenly.

The girl behind the counter was on the telephone talking to her boyfriend.

"How much is that doll?" I asked again, only louder.

The girl looked at me. "I gotta go now. Bye."

She took her out of the case and set her on the top of the counter. I straightened her cape and a ringlet that was falling into her face.

"Two hundred and fifty dollars. It's genuine porcelain."

"Oh." I swallowed. "Well. Thanks."

The girl put Amelia back into the case—crumpling the cape all over again—and picked up the telephone. Then she turned her back on me.

I looked at Amelia through the glass, holding those perfect little skates in that perfect little white hand. Two hundred and fifty dollars was a lot of money for a doll.

For anything. Me, I like bargains, and I'm pretty good at finding them. But suddenly I wanted Amelia no matter how much she cost. I hadn't wanted a doll since I was eight years old, but I wanted this one to put on my dresser so I could just look at her and touch the soft velvet of her cape every single day. I'd never owned anything so beautiful. So *perfect.*

Sinjian was running toward me, knocking toys off the shelves as he went. "Can we buy something, Gracie? Please!"

"I already told you no!" Even to me my voice sounded sharp.

Sinjian surprised me. He didn't whine or beg or cry. Instead, he looked at me very closely, and for just a minute he seemed a whole lot older than six years old. Maybe he would understand.

"See that doll?" I pointed.

Sinjian moved so close to the case that you could see his breath on the glass.

"Isn't she beautiful?" I practically whispered.

He studied her for a long time, absorbing the details of her hair, her face, her clothes.

"So what do you think?" I held my breath.

"I think dolls suck," he said.

Mom was up when we got back to the duplex. She was sitting at the kitchen table wearing the nylon nightgown covered with little pink flowers that she's had forever.

Pete was busy buttering a piece of toast. His hair kept falling into his face.

"Hi," Pete greeted us.

"Hi," Mom said in a thin voice.

"I'm just trying to get your mother here to eat something," Pete said, putting the piece of toast in front of her. She picked it up and nibbled on it, then put it down like it was too heavy for her to hold.

"I guess I'm not very hungry, Pete. I'm sorry."

"Did you two see something downtown you want? Something we can buy as soon as we strike it rich with Americalife?" Pete was using his happy voice. Mom tried to smile.

I held my breath, hoping Sinjian wouldn't say anything about the doll.

"Yeah! I want a new GI Joe. I want a trillion new GI Joes!"

"I hope you get all the GI Joes in the world," Mom said, trying to smile some more. "I hope you get all the GI Joes in the entire universe."

Sinjian laughed.

Mom shivered, even though the apartment was hot. "I think I'll go lie down for a while."

"Let me help you up," Pete said.

"I'm fine," Mom said, getting up. "Don't worry about me."

You're not fine. You're not.

Pete's face clouded as he watched her go to the bedroom.

"Gracie?" Pete sounded like he wanted to ask a question and I went stiff.

"What do you want?"

He looked at me, then shook his head. "Never mind."

Just then Sinjian started to sing. "My country 'tis of thee, I'm going to Germany—"

"Be quiet!" Pete snapped.

Sinjian flushed. "Geez. Geez! Everybody is always yelling at me in this stupid house. I miss Mom." He stomped off to our bedroom.

That left Pete and me. Pete had the look of a guy who's figured out he just barely missed the bus.

"I'm leaving for a little while, Gracie," he said. "Will you fix your mother something to eat in an hour or so?"

Pop! Something went off inside my head just like a firecracker. I'd already fixed dinner every night that week. I'd also poured cereal for breakfast, made sandwiches for lunch, washed and ironed clothes, and unpacked boxes. Boxes and boxes and boxes of Pete's life.

Pete kept talking. "I'm thinking your mom might—you know—that she might be—expecting a baby."

My mouth fell open, and Pete's face turned red.

"Well, it does happen, Gracie."

I started to laugh.

"This is just how Lily acted when she was first—expecting Sinjian. She was tired, she didn't eat, she cried all the time."

I kept laughing at how *stupid* Pete was, how he couldn't even say the word "pregnant."

He kept floundering. "I think a new baby would be great. I like babies."

"Has Mom told you she's pregnant?"

"Well, no."

"Take my word for it, Pete. She isn't pregnant."

Pete folded his arms and faced the kitchen. He stopped and looked straight at me.

I caught my breath. *He knows,* I thought. *He knows what's happening.*

I held my breath. The skin on my arms prickled with hope.

He can take her to the doctor. Get her pills. Make her take them.

"Pete—"

He suddenly looked down at the floor. "Be sure to make her eat something, Gracie."

He hurried out of the room.

Some things I just don't tell, not even to Sarah. Like the fear that I'm my mom all over again. When I saw her picture in Pete's yearbook, saw how happy she looked, my insides went dead cold. She was just a normal regular kid when she was my age.

I keep this fear like a hard little seed buried deep inside me. Mostly I ignore it.

But it's always there.

chapter 10

The next morning when I was doing the breakfast dishes, the doorbell rang.

"Nobody else is here," I told Sinjian, who was still picking at his bowl of Cheerios. "Will you please get that for me?" He groaned like I'd just asked him to take a bath. Sinjian hates baths. He also hates to brush his teeth and change his underwear.

The doorbell rang again. Sinjian finally got up and left the kitchen. "No fair! I always have to do everything around here."

"Right," I said. I got out a dish towel and started to dry the silverware.

"Gracie," Sinjian called a minute later. "Oh Gra-cie! There's some *boys* here to see you."

I dried my hands. It was probably the UPS man with another Americalife shipment.

I walked into the room and nearly died.

"Gracie's it, had a fit, kissed the boys in arithmetic . . ." Sinjian sang as he skipped out the front door.

Tiimo was standing there with another guy. Both of them were wearing running clothes and baseball caps on backward, but the friend was taller and a lot bigger through the shoulders and chest.

All I could think was I didn't have any mascara on.

"Hi, Gracie," said Tiimo. "This is Elroy Murphy—" His friend slugged him in the arm so hard that he stumbled backward.

"Pinhead!"

"Except that if you want to live you better call him Murph." Tiimo was laughing.

"Hi," I said.

"She ain't so talkative, is she?" Murph said. Already I didn't like him.

"Yeah? Well you talk too much." Tiimo slugged Murph and Murph slugged him back again. Have you ever noticed how guys are always punching each other around?

"Do you want to sit down?" I asked.

Tiimo and Murph sat on the couch, only they didn't just sit—they sort of draped their arms and legs everywhere and between the two of them, they filled up the whole couch.

"You sure have a lot of plants," said Tiimo. "I noticed that the other night."

"I like plants."

"Maybe you could give my mom some hints about keeping them alive."

"Your mom," said Murph, "looks at a plant and it shrivels up. When plants see your mother walk into the produce department at Smith's, they put their little plant paws over their eyes and scream, 'Oh noooo! It's Mrs. Lehtinen! *We're doomed!'*" Murph grabbed his own throat and made choking noises. Tiimo was laughing. He looked at me.

I couldn't believe how friendly he was being when he'd been so angry the other day.

"Anyway, we just got back from the D.G.," said Tiimo.

"The D.G.?" I hoped I didn't sound as stupid as I felt.

"Hey, she's new, Idiot," said Murph. "You gotta explain stuff to her." Would Murph always talk like I was in another room?

"D.G. stands for Deseret Gym," said Tiimo. "We were working out."

Murph flexed so that the muscles on his chest practically leaped out of his shirt. Tiimo laughed. "We're trying out for the football team this fall."

"That's great," I said, wishing I could stop thinking about the fact that I didn't have any mascara on. The three of us sat in silence for a couple of seconds. Murph looked at me, then at Tiimo, and back at me again.

"Anyway," said Tiimo, "I wanted to see if you were going to be around here about five this afternoon."

"I think so. Yes."

"I thought I'd come over again—if that's okay."

"That's great," I said for the second time.

Nobody spoke.

"Well, this has been loads of fun," said Murph. "I sincerely mean that."

Tiimo punched him. "We gotta go now, Gracie." He and Murph stood up and walked to the door. I followed them and saw two skateboards parked on the porch.

"See you later, Gracie."

"See you," I said.

As I watched them guide their skateboards up the street, I thought about the way Tiimo had said my name. I liked the way it sounded.

As soon as Tiimo turned the corner, I ran straight to the bathroom to put on my mascara. The tube was in the middle right-hand drawer, which is supposed to be *mine,* but Pete's beat-up old shave kit was sitting on top of all my things. I'm sure he just threw it in there without even noticing what he was doing. I put it where it belonged. Then I pulled out my mascara and began stroking my lashes with the wand.

Did Tiimo like the way I looked?

I spent the rest of the day just killing time—I looked at magazines, watched TV, made some cookies. Oatmeal with raisins.

Pete came home for part of the afternoon and tried to design a bumper sticker for Americalife products.

"Hey, Gracie," he said. "Since there are so many Mormons in Salt Lake City, I thought I'd go for the religious angle. What do you think about this?" He held up a piece

of paper with big lettering that said GOD IS OUR TOP DIS-
TRIBUTOR!

"It's awful!"

Pete looked hurt. "What do you mean awful?"

"I think it will offend people."

Pete looked at his piece of paper and frowned. "I don't
think it will offend anybody. I think it's kind of original."

"Fine. Don't ask my opinion next time. Do whatever
you want." I picked up a magazine and buried my face in
it.

By four thirty I had an upset stomach, the kind I used
to get right before Christmas when I was a little girl. What
could Tiimo want to see me about?

When it was almost five o'clock, I got out a plate and
put some cookies on it.

Five o'clock came. So did five five and five ten and
finally five twenty.

Maybe he'd forgotten.

Or maybe he'd really never planned to come in the first
place. He and Murph were just playing some kind of trick
on me.

The telephone rang. I snatched the receiver like it was
something on the Bargain Table.

"Hello?"

"Hi, Gracie." It was Tiimo.

"Oh. Hi." I tried very hard to sound normal.

"You probably noticed I'm not there yet."

I smiled a little. "Well, yeah. I did notice."

"I'm baby-sitting, if you can believe it."

I probably wouldn't have if I hadn't heard a little kid crying in the background.

"Mom does day-care at home," Tiimo said. "She and Mummi—that's my grandmother—had to run to the grocery store, and they're not back yet."

"Oh," I said. "That's okay. Another time maybe."

"Why don't you come up here? I need to explain something to you about the Americalife meeting."

I said fine, so Tiimo gave me his address. He lived on O Street, too.

When I got off the phone, I found a little plastic bag and put the cookies in it. Then I left a note for Pete, telling him to pick up Sinjian, who was playing at a park at the end of M Street.

It was hot outside, probably close to one hundred degrees. I had to blink a few times before my eyes got used to the sunlight.

O Street is lined with old houses—some of them huge, some of them small. Tiimo's house was little, made out of brick, painted white.

I walked up to the front porch and rang the doorbell. Inside a dog barked. I heard people running toward the door.

"Move over you guys," Tiimo said. "I'll get it." When he opened the door, he was surrounded by five little kids who were staring at me with their mouths wide open. A big red dog pushed through them and started waving its tail like a flag.

"Hi, Gracie!" Tiimo swung open the screen door and let me in. The dog sniffed my legs.

"Leave her alone, Jessica," said Tiimo to the dog. Jessica gave me one last embarrassing sniff then walked to the middle of the room and plopped down in the middle of the floor. The kids started crawling all over her like a bunch of ants on an anthill.

"She's pretty patient," I said.

"She just loves abuse." Tiimo and I smiled at each other.

"Here. These are for you." I handed him the bag of cookies.

He took one out of the bag and ate it, then passed the rest around to the kids. "These are great!"

I looked around the room. Although there were toys scattered all over the floor, everything was very clean. There was a big bulletin board on the wall over the couch, filled with calendars and things that had been made by little kids. A good smell came from the kitchen. I noticed five plants on the windowsill—all of them dead except for one, and it was nearly gone, too.

I sat down in a rocking chair that had a big green afghan spread neatly across its back. Tiimo sat down across from me. A little boy with bright orange hair and freckles crawled into his lap.

"Thanks for coming over," he said while he wrestled with the kid, who was screaming with laughter.

"Does your mom baby-sit this many kids every day?"

"Yeah. She's a licensed day-care provider. In Finland

she made pretty good money doing this, but here in the States being a day-care provider isn't even considered a real job. Taking care of people's kids is something you do if you aren't qualified to do anything else." Suddenly he seemed more like the Tiimo who'd come to my house for the meeting.

"Why did she leave Finland?"

"She and Mummi joined the Mormon Church when I was a baby. My grandfather was dead and Mom was divorced, so it was just the three of us. When I was three, we all moved to Zion. I know she had this dream that life in America would be perfect." He gave me a wry smile. "For my sake I'm glad she came. But sometimes I think she'd have been better off if she'd stayed in Helsinki. Things haven't worked out that great for her here." He shrugged.

Suddenly Tiimo turned to the kids and said, "Hey, guys! Tell Gracie who lives in Finland!"

"Joulupuuki!!" They were laughing.

"And who's Joulupuuki?" Tiimo asked.

"Santa Claus!" They all shouted together.

"Americans are confused about that," Tiimo explained. "They think he lives at the North Pole. I like to set the record straight whenever I get the chance."

I laughed and kept looking at Tiimo, hoping he wouldn't catch me staring. My heart was beating faster.

"I wanted to explain why I wasn't very friendly when I came to your apartment that day." He started tying the shoelace of the little boy in his lap.

"You don't have to explain anything."

He went on like he hadn't heard. "Mom is always looking for new ways to make a little bit extra here and there, but she doesn't always make such smart decisions. Know what I mean?"

I knew.

"Anyway," he said, "I just try to look out for her."

"Well, there's something I wanted to explain to you," I said suddenly. "Pete isn't my real dad. He's my stepfather."

Tiimo looked at me closely. "You mentioned that, the first time I was at your place."

"Did I?" My face went red.

He was still looking at me.

"Hey, Tiimo," screamed one of the little boys, "give me five!"

Tiimo did. Then he turned to me again and said, "Maybe we could do something together sometime. Get pizza. Go to a movie."

I kept my voice calm. "Yeah. That would be fun."

We talked for a while after that, mostly about movies we'd both seen, but also about the high school here. He told me which classes to take, which ones to avoid, things a new person ought to know.

The whole time I sat in his living room, watching little kids crawl in and out of his lap, I kept thinking how easy it was to talk to him. Usually, I turn quiet around boys. "You are so weird," Sarah always says. "Don't you want a boyfriend?" Actually, I would. I spend a lot of time thinking about how *nice* it would be to like someone who feels the same way about me. But whenever anybody starts to show interest, I pull away. Practically everything I know about kissing comes from sitting in the cab of a truck while Sarah's in the back making out.

"Well," I said finally, "I gotta go home and fix dinner."

"I'll give you a call," he said as we walked to the door.

I nodded. "Look, why don't I take that plant in the window home and see if I can—" I stopped. Here I was, insulting his mother's plant.

"—raise it from the dead?" Tiimo finished my sentence.

"Something like that," I mumbled quickly.

He laughed, then took the plant from the windowsill and handed it to me.

"Thanks," he said.

"Thanks to you, too. For setting me straight."

Tiimo's eyebrows raised like question marks.

"About Santa Claus."

Tiimo smiled as he shut the door behind me. "See you later, Gracie."

chapter 11

I looked at Mrs. Lehtinen's fern on the bookcase where I'd put it the day before.

I'm pretty amazed by people who say they can't grow things. You don't have to be a genius. All you have to do is figure out what the plant needs and then give it what it wants. I pinched off everything dead on Mrs. Lehtinen's plant, then cut back the rest with a pair of scissors. I put it on the bookcase where it won't get a lot of direct sunlight. That was Mrs. Lehtinen's problem. She had it sitting right there in a west window. Ferns just hate too much light.

Sinjian was sitting on the couch, watching television—*Family Feud.*

"Turn it down, please," I said.

Sinjian didn't move. He completely loses touch with reality when he's in front of the television.

"You'll wake up Mom," I said, louder this time.

Sinjian screamed an answer at the screen.

The doorbell rang. I marched past Sinjian, turning the TV off as I walked toward the door.

"Hey!" said Sinjian.

Two men stood on our front porch. One was thin and middle-aged with skin the color of bread dough. The other was younger and heavier. They had the same face, though, with the same sweaty upper lip, so I figured they were father and son.

"Can I help you?"

The older one cleared his throat. "Uh—are you the lady of the house?"

"No," I said, watching both of them carefully.

The skinny one straightened up and said, "We're here to collect your freezer—the one you folks bought before you skipped American Fork."

He was talking about the freezer Pete gave Mom for their wedding.

"We didn't *skip* American Fork." My mind was racing in circles, like a dog chasing its own tail. Did Pete make arrangements with these guys to pick it up? Did it need to be repaired? "Is there something wrong with it?"

"Yeah," the younger one grunted with a laugh. "It ain't paid for!"

"Shut up, LaMont." The older man turned to me. "We're on a repo, Sweetheart." He shoved some official-looking papers in my face.

I thought my knees might give out. "I need to talk to my mom about this."

"Ain't nothin' to ask her about," said Skinny. "You no payee, you no keepee."

"Stay here." I locked the screen door so they couldn't come in.

I finally had Sinjian's attention. "What's the matter, Gracie? What's happening?"

"Be quiet. Don't let them in."

I walked straight into the bedroom with Sinjian at my heels.

"Mom, there are some men here about the freezer. They say they're going to repossess it."

She didn't move.

"Mom?"

She sat up, then sank into her pillow again.

"I can't deal with that right now," she said in a small weak voice. "Tell them to please come back when Pete's home."

Everything inside of me began to churn.

"I don't think they'll go away . . ." I was practically whining, just like I used to when I was little. "Please, Mom." Sinjian was hovering behind me in the doorway, driving me crazy. "Please."

"Not now, Baby." Mom's voice was fading.

My hands were shaking, and I thought I might throw up.

"It'll be okay," Mom said. "Pete will take care of things later."

"But, Mom. *Please.*"

She rolled over.

116

"Come on, Sinjian." We left Mom's room and I slammed the door hard behind me. I hoped the noise would make her head hurt.

"What's wrong with her, Gracie?" Sinjian was in my face. "I don't like her anymore. I did at first but now I think she's weird."

I went cold with fury.

"Don't you ever say that to me again," I snapped.

The two men were still standing on the front porch.

"My mom says for you to come back later when my stepfather is home."

"Yeah," said Sinjian, his nose pressed flat against the screen door.

"Hey, Sweetheart," said the older man, ignoring Sinjian, "you'll save us both a whole lot of trouble if you just let us in now."

"Maybe. Maybe not. Come back later."

"Next time it will be the constable here!" said Skinny. I shut the door in their faces. They stood on the porch talking, and after a minute, they left.

"What's happening?" Sinjian asked.

I didn't answer. I just walked straight into the kitchen and started to empty dry dishes out of the drainer. I put up the plates first, then the cups. Then the silverware in perfect order—knife, spoon, fork. Knife, spoon, fork. They clanked against each other as I dropped them into the drawer. *Knife, spoon, fork. Knife, spoon, fork.*

"Gracie! Gracie! Gracie—"

"Leave me alone, Sinjian. Run outside."

Knife, spoon, fork . . .

I shut the top drawer and walked to the living room. I sat down in the rocking chair Mom and I had had for as long as I could remember. I took the afghan and draped it around my shoulders even though the house was filled with July heat. Then I rocked back and forth, back and forth.

In my mind, I saw Mrs. Macleod that day in her kitchen trying to make me feel better.

Good things can come from change.

The room started to go dark because my eyes were filled with tears.

chapter 12

When Sarah called the other day—she always calls in the middle of the day even though the rates are high—I told her about Tiimo and Murph.

"This Jimbo has been coming over with his friend every morning?" she said.

"His name is Tiimo," I told her.

"Whatever."

"Anyway they always stop by on their way home from the gym."

"Both of them?"

"Yeah. We sit out on the front porch and talk. Also, Tiimo and I listen to Murph insult Mrs. Burns's cat. He calls her Flatface and Princess Hairball. Stuff like that."

"Do these guys both like you or something?" Sarah asked.

I didn't know. I like it when Tiimo and Murph stop by although I'm not sure what it means exactly when two boys come together.

"Maybe they think I'm one of the guys."

"Maybe." Sarah yawned.

I wanted to tell her how I thought about Tiimo whenever I did the dishes or folded the clothes and especially when I drifted off to sleep every night, but I could tell she was already bored with our conversation, something that was happening to us more and more.

"Come live with me," said Sarah. "I've been totally depressed ever since you left."

I didn't say anything. The word "depressed" stopped me short.

"I hate my mom," she was saying. "She's always trying to tell me what to do."

My mom never told me what to do these days.

"I gotta go. Sinjian's crying," I lied.

The next morning I was vacuuming the living room carpet when the doorbell rang.

It was Tiimo and Murph, only they had Sinjian with them. He was crying. His eye was red and starting to swell.

"Does this belong to you?" Murph asked, shoving Sinjian through the door at me.

"Sinjian! What happened?"

"Put some ice on it," said Tiimo, letting himself and Murph in.

"This guy thinks he's a stinking doctor," said Murph.

I led Sinjian into the kitchen and started filling a plastic bag with ice cubes.

"What happened?" I asked again. "Did you fall down?"

Murph snorted. "Get real."

"I think someone hit him," said Tiimo, touching the skin around Sinjian's eye carefully.

"Ouch!" Sinjian jumped like his feet were on fire.

"Did the kids up the street do that to you?" I asked.

Sinjian nodded miserably.

"I told you to leave them alone!"

"Excellent sister you got there, pal," said Murph, rooting through the kitchen cupboards for something to eat. "Yells at you when you get hurt. I like that in a woman."

I glared at the back of Murph's head. But he was right. Why was I yelling at Sinjian because he was going to have a black eye?

Tiimo took the bag of ice from me and pressed it against Sinjian's face. He flinched a little, but he let Tiimo take care of him.

"Is he going to be okay?" I asked.

"Hey," said Tiimo. "Trust me."

"It wasn't my fault," said Sinjian, his voice shifting into a high-pitched whine. "I just told them that I know Michael Jackson . . ."

Murph groaned.

"It's true!" Sinjian screamed.

"Rule Number One for Living, Kid," Murph said. "Don't be a dork."

Tiimo laughed. "It's our personal motto."

"We learned it in Boy Scouts," said Murph. "Love your country and don't be a dork."

"Let's go outside." Tiimo gave Sinjian his hand.

"Right. Let's find those little creeps that decked you and make them mow grass with their teeth."

Sinjian started to smile as he followed Murph and Tiimo through the living room and out the front door.

The four of us sat down on the porch steps. Already the sun hung like a hot white ball in the middle of the sky.

"We're going to fry again today," said Tiimo.

"Take me away," moaned Murph. "I don't want to live in Utah no more!"

"Look, Gracie," said Sinjian pointing to Mrs. Burns's empty porch. "I think Tatiana is loose again."

"Good," said Murph. "I hope she gets flattened by a truck."

Sinjian looked worried.

"Don't worry. Tatiana's fine," I said. I couldn't believe he still cared what happened to that cat after the way Mrs. Burns had treated him.

Murph and Tiimo started talking about football. On the one hand they acted like I wasn't even there, since they never asked me what I thought. On the other hand I could tell they were both checking to see if I was listening. From the way Murph was talking, you'd think he was good enough to have a couple of Super Bowl rings sitting in his top drawer at home.

"Hey, there she is!" Sinjian was pointing to a lilac

bush. Tatiana was crouching beneath it, getting ready to pounce.

"She's gonna get that bird!" Sinjian was on his feet now.

It was a lime green bird with a light orange face.

"Some kind of a parrot," said Murph. "Parrots are the state bird of Utah, Sinjian. Did you know that, huh?"

"We gotta stop her," said Sinjian, scrambling off the porch. "No, Tatiana!"

She sprang just like a long jumper from the mark and landed right on the bird.

"No!" screamed Sinjian.

Tatiana had the bird, squawking and screeching, in her mouth now. Tiimo was right behind Sinjian, who jumped on Tatiana. The bird popped out of her mouth like a cork out of a champagne bottle at Christmas.

"Get it! Get it!" yelled Sinjian, hanging onto Tatiana, who was squirming and meowing.

Tiimo scooped up the bird, which was either too stunned or too hurt to move.

"You get off my cat immediately!" Mrs. Burns was on her front porch in a housecoat and curlers.

"It's okay, Sinjian. I got it," Tiimo said.

Sinjian let go of Tatiana, who scampered across the lawn and through Mrs. Burns's open screen door.

"I *warned* you," she screeched at Sinjian, "and now you're going to be very sorry! I'm calling the police right this very instant!"

She spun around and marched inside.

"Say, I really love your outfit!" Murph called after her. Sinjian was shaking.

"Don't mind her," Tiimo said, stroking the bird's head. "The police will know she's nuts."

"Yeah," said Murph, "especially when she tells them that you were molesting her cat."

Tiimo handed Sinjian the bird. It nestled against his chest.

"Can we keep it, Gracie?"

"It looks like the kind of bird that belongs to somebody," I said doubtfully.

"Please—"

"We don't have a cage."

"We do," said Murph. "We used to have a bird before it decided to die on us."

Sinjian looked at me again. Something about his swollen eye and the gentle way he held the bird started to get to me.

"Let me think about it."

"Tell you what," said Tiimo, "let's you and me and Murph get the cage, then go to Western Garden to buy some bird seed. Is that okay with you, Gracie?" Tiimo turned to me.

I nodded. They waved and left, Sinjian still holding the bird carefully against his chest.

"It's a peach-faced lovebird," Sinjian told me later. "We saw the same kind at Western Garden." He was peeling a carrot to put in the cage. I watched him take slow perfect sweeps with the carrot peeler. Most kids his age would probably have had a carrot full of nicks by the time they finished—that is if they could even manage to peel one in the first place. Not Sinjian. His carrot would be smooth and clean. He was good with those long thin hands of his. Good enough to draw detailed pictures of imaginary worlds. Sometimes he sat at the table in the living room and drew for hours, making action sounds with his mouth and having conversations with himself like he was actually fifty different people in the same room.

Sinjian shows me everything he draws. At first I used to say, "Yeah, that's good," just so he'd stop bugging me. Then I started to notice that they really *were* good.

"Do you like Tiimo?" Sinjian asked. The carrot was completely peeled now.

"Don't leave the carrot peeler on the counter. Put it in the sink. Yes. I like Tiimo just fine."

I thought he would start to sing something stupid like "Gracie loves Tiimo!"

"I like him, too," he said thoughtfully. "I think I'll be a football player—just like Tiimo."

"He doesn't play football yet," I reminded Sinjian. "He has to make the team first, remember."

But he wasn't even listening. He was too busy telling me what a great quarterback he was going to be someday.

Just like Tiimo.

chapter 13

~~~~~~~~~~ ◆

Sinjian was standing in front of the bird's cage the next morning, holding a book in his hand.

"What do you call the world's scariest fish?" He emphasized every single syllable.

The bird bobbed its head, then scuttled on its perch from side to side.

"Jack the Kipper."

I laughed. It was *so* stupid.

Sinjian looked up at me confused. "I don't get it."

"Jack the Kipper rhymes with Jack the Ripper."

He gave me a blank look.

"Never mind," I said. I walked over to him and looked at the cover of his book. It was called *101 Jokes for Kids*.

"I didn't know you could read," I said.

He shrugged.

"That's pretty good, Sinjian," I said. "You haven't even been to first grade yet."

When I was in the first grade I didn't know for sure if *S*

came before *T* in the alphabet, and I was too embarrassed to ask my teacher about it.

Sinjian flipped the page. "Why is a chef the meanest person in the kitchen?"

"Because he beats the eggs and whips the cream," I said.

Sinjian was impressed.

"I remember that joke from when I was a kid," I said.

"Anyways, Tiimo gave me this book for keeps," he said. "I'm going to read it to Dr. Seuss every single day so he won't get lonely and die."

"You named your bird Dr. Seuss?" I asked.

"Dr. Seuss-on-the-loose," he said, pretty pleased with himself for coming up with a rhyme.

I laughed. "Very good, Sinjian."

The mail dropped through the front-door slot.

"Yes!" Sinjian raced to the pile of mail. He sorted through the envelopes one by one, then threw them down on the floor.

"Sinjian!"

He folded his arms and threw his chin out.

Then it hit me. He was looking for a letter from his mother. She hadn't written once since we moved to Salt Lake. Anger swelled up in me like a balloon.

The bird squawked.

"I think Dr. Seuss wants you to tell him some more jokes."

He shuffled to the cage and started to read. "Did you hear about the vampire who went to sea?"

Lily! *Damn* her.

"Dr. Seuss?" Murph snorted when Sinjian told him and Tiimo later that day. "What kind of a stupid name is that? It sounds like something Mr. Rogers would name a bird." Murph started talking to the bird through the bars of its cage. "People are gonna think you're a real wimp with a name like that. If you were my bird, I'd call you Arnold. Arnold the Terminator."

Sinjian looked unhappy.

"Wimp, wimp, wimp," said Murph.

"At least his name isn't Elroy," said Tiimo, giving Murph a little shove. Then he picked up Sinjian and threw him over a shoulder like a bag of potatoes. Sinjian squealed with laughter.

"He's been making fliers to post around the neighborhood. If no one claims the bird then Sinjian can keep him," I said.

"Come on," said Tiimo, "we'll help you."

Tiimo, Murph, and Sinjian sat at the kitchen table and began making posters that said: FOUND! ONE MAN-EATING PARROT! CALL 555-6487.

I watched the three of them as I started to mix up some cookie dough. Gingersnap. It was pretty terrific of Tiimo and Murph to be so nice to Sinjian, who didn't have any friends here yet. I wondered if he had many friends in California—besides Michael Jackson. He didn't talk about them if he did. He didn't talk much about Lily either except when he was throwing a fit, and then he'd say things like, "I'm going to run away from here and live with Mom."

Only I think he knew in his heart that Lily wouldn't have him.

Suddenly I felt my own heart beat hard against my chest.

A shaft of morning sun coming through the kitchen window hit Sinjian just like a spotlight. He looked pale and small and skinny sitting there between Murph and Tiimo. As skinny as the wild cat I used to feed but never touched.

Don't you hate it? The way some adults treat their kids without even thinking about it?

"Let's take these around now," said Tiimo, gathering up the fliers. "Come with us, Gracie."

I looked at the bowlful of dough waiting to be spooned onto a cookie sheet.

"Please," said Tiimo.

I put the bowl in the fridge.

We took the fliers all over the neighborhood and posted them on telephone poles, in coin laundries, in grocery stores, and on the bulletin board of the Avenues branch library.

"Don't be too unhappy if the real owner calls," I kept warning Sinjian. I didn't think I could stand to see his face when that happened.

"Always looking on the bright side," said Murph, throwing a tennis ball he found in the gutter to Tiimo. "I really like that in a woman."

I decided that *obnoxious* was the word that best described Murph.

"Lighten up, Gracie," he said. "Geez. You're so uptight all the time."

"No I'm not," I said. "I'm not."

"Yes you are. You definitely are."

I laughed at Murph like he was crazy, but I could feel my cheeks go pink.

"If you don't watch out you're going to turn into Mrs. Burns," Murph said. "You're gonna start tying up cats so people won't snatch them. You're gonna stand on your porch in a housecoat screaming at kids to stay off your property." He struck a pose like Mrs. Burns—one hand on his hip, the other pointing in the air—and called in a high, shrill voice. *"You damn kids better stay off my property or I'm gonna rub peas in your hair!"* Murph laughed. "That's what my grandma always used to say to us. She was gonna do that if we did something bad. Grandma was kind of weird."

I blinked hard. I could feel Tiimo watching me. He threw the tennis ball at Murph's chest. "Shut up," he said easily.

"Anyways," said Sinjian, "Gracie doesn't even have a cat."

I slowed down so that I was walking a foot or so behind everybody.

Was I really going to turn into Mrs. Burns? Was I going to stand on my side of the duplex and scare people away?

I felt a little twist inside my chest.

We got back from the library just as a beatup blue truck that looked vaguely familiar pulled away from the curb in front of our duplex. The palms of my hands felt clammy. Something bad was happening.

"Maybe you guys better go home now," I said.

Tiimo gave me a close look but Murph said, "Hell no. I want some cookies." Then he barged into the house. Tiimo, Sinjian, and I followed him.

Pete was sitting on the couch when we walked through the front door. His face was sweaty and red, and he was breathing heavily.

"Where have you two been?" he snapped as though Tiimo and Murph weren't in the same room with us. I could feel Sinjian stiffen by my side.

Don't you dare scream at me in front of Tiimo.

"We were taking fliers about the bird around the neighborhood," I said.

"That damn bird!" Pete was getting redder and spraying spit through the air. "There are bird seeds all over the place. Feathers and bird seed!"

Since when did you care about a mess?

"I'll sweep it up," I said as lightly as I could.

Please, please just don't embarrass me now . . .

Sinjian darted into the kitchen, ducking his head as he ran past Pete. Tiimo and Murph stood still.

Pete got up from the couch and started to pace. First he tucked his hands under his armpits, then he shoved them deep into his pockets.

"Damn!" he kept mumbling to himself.

Suddenly I remembered the blue truck. It belonged to the men with the same face, the ones who came for our freezer. Just thinking about them made me shake.

"They came back, didn't they."

Pete glanced at me, then down at the floor, looking just like a kid who's been caught doing something wrong.

"You *said* you would take care of it!" I could hear my voice climb straight to the ceiling.

"I thought things were going to work out—"

"That's the problem with people like you! You always think things are going to work out, so you sit back and do nothing at all!"

Crash! The sound of shattering glass came from the kitchen.

Pete barreled straight into the kitchen.

I caught Tiimo's eyes, then looked away. Why had I lost my temper with Pete like that in front of Tiimo?

"Look at this," Pete was saying, "orange juice all over the floor! How can you be so stupid?"

Sinjian started to cry.

"I didn't mean that," Pete took a long deep breath. "Please stop crying."

My cheeks flamed as Sinjian ran to our room, and

Tiimo and Murph let themselves quietly out the front door.

I turned on Pete. "Don't call Sinjian stupid, because he isn't. And while you're at it, why don't you get in touch with that mother of his and tell her to write him a letter!"

As I walked out of the room I heard Pete say, "Yes. I will."

Tiimo called me the next morning.

"I'm sorry you had to be here when all that happened between Pete and me," I told him.

"Forget it," he said. "Do you know what day this is?"

"Tuesday?"

"July twenty-third."

"Oh," I said, not understanding. "Right."

He laughed. "We're coming to pick you up tonight at ten. Be ready, Gracie. Be ready . . ." Tiimo hung up.

Ten o'clock. Where would Tiimo and Murph be taking me at such a late hour? Mom and Pete were going to be at an Americalife meeting. Sinjian would be asleep.

Should I stay home just in case he woke up?

No!

He'd be fine. When ten o'clock struck, I'd be ready.

A horn blared out front.

I parted the drapes and saw a car. Tiimo was hanging out of the passenger seat window, waving for me to join them.

"Hi, Gracie!" he yelled when I ran outside. He opened

his door. I poked my head inside. The car was full of kids
—girls and boys both.

"I guess you'll just have to sit on my lap," Tiimo said.

Murph started whistling from somewhere deep in the
backseat of the car, and I turned red, but I sat on Tiimo's
lap.

"Hey, everybody, this is Gracie," said Tiimo, slipping
his arms easily around my waist. There was a chorus of
hellos.

"And these are just some guys from the neighborhood," Tiimo said. "We're going downtown to check out
the crowds."

"People camp out on the sidewalks to get good seats
for the parade tomorrow morning," someone said.

"Total morons," Murph said.

So that was it. Tomorrow was the twenty-fourth of
July. Pioneer Day, which is a big deal in Utah. I'd seen
the Salt Lake parade before on television.

"People *sleep* on the sidewalks?" I asked.

"They bring sleeping bags and lawn chairs and some
people even bring tents," a girl said.

"Yeah, but nobody gets much sleep," Tiimo told me.

A song came on the radio and Murph started to sing
along with it—just like Sarah always does.

"Shut up," everyone in the car yelled at the same time.

I felt Tiimo's hard legs beneath mine and his warm
breath on my skin. He smelled good, like he'd just taken
a shower and splashed something on afterward. I was

glad that the car was dark and that no one could tell I was blushing.

I thought about the first time I met Tiimo, how angry he was and how he even scared me a little. I didn't feel that way now.

"Main Street!" announced Chuck, the driver.

There were people everywhere, up and down the street, as far as I could see. Babies, old people, kids, couples, families. They were talking, walking around, chasing each other. A few were even watching television on little portable sets they held in their laps. Somebody was barbequing hamburgers on a grill standing on the sidewalk in front of Nordstrom's department store. The sound of firecrackers going off filled the night air.

Chuck pulled over, then told us where and what time to meet if we wanted a ride home. Everyone piled out of the car. Murph put his arm around a girl's shoulders and started to sing the song he'd just heard on the radio. He and Sarah would make a good pair.

"Is that Murph's girlfriend?" I asked. She was tall and very tan, with warm brown hair and eyes and the prettiest smile I'd ever seen. The way she looked and the way she moved reminded me of the does I used to see in the hills above American Fork.

"He wishes." Tiimo laughed. "Her name is Jill and she's friends with everybody. You ought to see her play tennis."

For a little while everyone stayed together, looking at the people and the store window displays, but after a while the group drifted apart, and Tiimo and I were alone.

"Look at that," he said, pointing at the sky.

A huge bunch of balloons—green, pink, yellow, blue—drifted lazily toward a bright half moon.

"It looks like—magic," I murmured.

Tiimo looked at me hard and I turned my head away. "It does," he answered softly.

We walked slowly down the sidewalk, threading our way through the crowds of people. A warm breeze blew up from the street, lifting my hair. I remembered the way Tiimo's breath felt on my back when I sat on his lap.

"There's a mini-park behind that building," said Tiimo. "Let's go there."

The park was a small lot tucked between two buildings, planted with grass and flowers. A couple making out on a blanket ignored us as we walked by and sat on a bench.

Even though I'd been talking to Tiimo every day for the past few weeks, I couldn't think of anything to say now that we were alone. I looked at the couple on the ground while Tiimo softly whistled the song Murph had been singing earlier.

"When does football practice start?" There. I'd found a question.

"Soon," Tiimo answered. "The first part of August."

Silence again except for the music from the street. Someone was playing the steel drums.

"Gracie," said Tiimo, "have you ever really wanted

something? I mean *really* wanted it?" His voice was tight, intense.

I thought of the perfect porcelain doll—Amelia—with the blue cape and tiny skates.

"Yes," I said slowly, "but I doubt I'll get it."

Tiimo looked surprised. Almost shocked.

"If you wanted it bad enough you would. You would!" The light from his eyes was hard and bright.

"I don't know about that really—"

He folded his arms across his chest, leaned back against the bench, and looked at the sky.

"I think if you want something bad enough, you can figure out a way to get it. You'll work twice as hard as the other guys—lift more weights, run more wind sprints, learn the plays faster than anybody else—and in the end you'll get what you want, what you *deserve.* I really do believe that." His voice was low and tight, like a coiled spring.

I looked at the sky, too. Maybe he was right. Maybe if I wanted the doll bad enough I could find a way to get it. Baby-sit. Clean other ladies' houses. Get a job at a fast-food place, even though I was technically underage. Still, I didn't know—

"You gotta have faith, Gracie," Tiimo said. Then he laughed. "Sorry. Sometimes I get a little *intense.*"

I looked at him again.

What a strange person you are. Funny, gentle with kids, happy to take a backseat to Murph. But something else, too.

I shivered.

Fierce.

"Are you cold?" Tiimo asked. "Because I can fix that." He put his arm around my shoulders and pulled me close to him. I could hear my own heartbeat.

The warm air was filled with the scent of sweet alyssum and petunias and even faraway pine trees from the mountains surrounding the valley. Suddenly everything seemed perfect. The city. The night. Tiimo and I together.

"Gracie—"

I turned to face him, my lips nearly brushing his.

"Hey, Tiimo!" It was Murph.

Tiimo swore under his breath, and I laughed nervously. We pulled away from each other.

Murph and Jill were running across the street toward us.

"Did we interrupt something?" Murph laughed as Jill slugged him in the arm. Tiimo glared at them.

"One of the guys said they saw you two come down here," said Jill in a voice that sounded like an apology. She gave me a friendly smile. "Do you want to go get something to eat with us?"

I quickly tucked a loose strand of hair behind my ear and stood up without looking at Tiimo. "Yeah. That would be great."

"I'm *really* sorry," Jill whispered in my ear as the four of us were walking down Main Street.

I was sorry, too.

*   *   *

I got home about one in the morning.

Pete, Sinjian, and Mom were waiting up for me on the couch. Sinjian was curled up tightly next to his father's side. Pete had an arm around his shoulders. Mom looked nervous.

"Where the *hell* have you been?" His face was as red and round as a balloon and the words escaped from his mouth in a whoosh.

I looked at Mom. She dropped her eyes.

"I just went downtown with a couple of kids," I said, looking straight at Pete again. "I thought it would be okay. You and Mom were gone and Sinjian was asleep—"

"It's after midnight, Gracie! When we came home, Sinjian was hysterical because he thought you left him."

"But he was asleep when I left," I said lamely. "I just thought—"

"You didn't think," snapped Pete. "That's the problem! You didn't think to leave a note to tell him or us where you were going. You didn't think how your brother would feel if he woke up alone in an empty house."

I felt a stab of guilt as I looked at Sinjian's wide eyes.

But here's the thing. I didn't like the way Pete—*Pete,* the Crown Prince of Stupid—was telling me that I'd done something wrong when he made a career out of doing stupid things.

And I also didn't like the way Mom sat next to him on the couch, looking at the floor, folding her shaking hands like a little girl, instead of defending me. The blood began pounding behind my eyes.

"Anyway, Sinjian isn't my brother," I said. "And you are definitely not my father." Then I turned and walked straight out of the room. But not until I'd seen Sinjian's face.

He looked like he'd been slapped.

chapter 14

I was still mad at Mom and Pete when I woke up the next morning, but when I thought about Sinjian's face, I wanted to pull the sheet up way over my head and hide.

It was Pete's fault. If he hadn't accused me of being stupid, I would have never said what I did.

The floor groaned loudly beneath my feet when I crawled out of bed.

Sinjian was already in the kitchen, pouring himself a bowl of cold cereal.

"Why don't I fix you some waffles," I said.

He kept pouring the cereal.

"Or French toast. I make great French toast, Sinjian. Do you know why? Because I mix just a little orange juice into the egg batter. It's like a secret ingredient."

He splashed milk into his bowl.

I started filling the sink with hot water and soap so I could do up last night's dishes.

"Did you have a nightmare last night?" I asked, trying to sound as friendly as possible. "Is that why you woke up?"

Sinjian shrugged his shoulders and shoveled more cereal into his mouth.

"I used to have nightmares all the time when I was your age. Once I dreamed that my Halloween costume came to life and started chasing me around the backyard." I laughed a little.

Sinjian kept right on eating as though he hadn't heard me. I turned off the tap, pulled out a bar stool, and sat down next to him. I reached out and touched his hair.

"Your hair needs to be combed. Why don't you get a comb and squirt bottle as soon as you finish eating and let me do it for you."

"I combed it already yesterday," he said.

"Look," I said, "I'm sorry about what I said last night."

Sinjian crunched his cereal for a while. "It's okay, Gracie," he finally said in a flat little voice, "I already knew that I wasn't really your brother."

Something inside of me turned over.

"Anyways I'm a real ninja," he added, "and ninjas are always orphans."

"Ninjas are not always orphans. They can have families, too."

"You don't know everything," said Sinjian. "You think you do, but you don't."

Panic began to prick my stomach like a little pin.

142

"We can watch the parade on TV after you finish eating," I said.

Sinjian didn't answer. And he didn't watch the parade with me either.

Jill Tanner called me that afternoon.

"We've got a pool," she said. "Why don't you come over about three o'clock and we'll go swimming, okay? My sisters and their friends will be here. And who knows? My brother and some of his fraternity brothers might stagger down from the university to join us."

I was smiling as I hung up. It would be nice to have a girlfriend again.

Jill lived on the east side of Virginia Street which is about six blocks away from O. One of the interesting things about this neighborhood is that it is a real mix of people who have money and people who don't. One look at the Tanners' big Victorian house surrounded by rose gardens, and I knew it would be hard to invite her to the duplex.

"Gracie!" Jill said when she opened the front door. "Come in!"

Inside, the wood floors were covered with oriental rugs, and bookshelves lined the walls. Antique furniture —chairs, end tables, sofas, and a big piano—was everywhere. It didn't feel like a museum, though, because shoes and cups and newspapers were scattered around.

"Hey, Mom!" Jill called. "Come here!"

A woman as tall as Jill walked into the living room, wiping her hands on a dish towel.

"Mom, this is Gracie. Gracie, this is Mom." Jill gave her a big kiss on the cheek. "You can call her Delores."

Delores smiled. "Sorry this place is such a wreck. I didn't plan on cleaning house on my day off"—she shot a look at Jill, who shrugged—"but maybe I'll have to after all."

"Let's go upstairs and change," Jill said.

Jill had her own bedroom and there were trophies, framed ribbons, and posters of tennis stars everywhere. A racket stood next to a pile of romance novels by the door.

"Tiimo said you're a really terrific tennis player."

"I love to play," Jill said as she disappeared into her own bathroom to change. "I want to turn pro someday."

Something on the top of her dresser caught my attention. There were three porcelain dolls sitting in a group, looking lost and out of place among the tennis trophies. One was dressed like Little Red Riding Hood, one like Alice in Wonderland, the last like Cinderella in her ball gown. Each was as beautiful as the doll I saw that day at Busy Bee Toys.

I walked toward the dresser, then touched the face of Little Red Riding Hood. It felt cool and clean beneath my warm fingers.

"Do you collect dolls?" Jill asked me as she walked back into the bedroom, adjusting one of her swimming suit straps.

I shook my head.

"I don't either really. My mom's the one who likes them. She gives me and Kate and Meg one every Christmas. I've got tons more in the closet." Jill joined me at the dresser and looked at the dolls like she hadn't seen them for a while. "I think Mom sometimes wishes I liked the same things she did—pretty dolls, music, school." She laughed.

"What does your dad do?" I asked casually while adding up in my head just how much three porcelain dolls every Christmas must cost.

"He's an attorney. So's Mom. What does yours do?"

"He died when I was little." Jill shot me a sympathetic look. "My stepfather is—in sales."

"Oh. That's neat," Jill said without much interest as if she didn't care much what people's fathers did. I suddenly felt better.

"Let's go outside," she said. "We can talk while we're waiting for everybody else to get here."

To say that Jill and I went swimming would be technically incorrect since we never actually went into the pool. Instead we sat on the deck, rubbing lots of baby oil on our legs and talking about boys.

"Is Murph—you know—your boyfriend?"

"*Murph?*" She laughed just like I'd told her a very funny joke. "No. We're just good friends."

Good friends. Did guys ever say things like that about girls? Somehow I doubted it.

"You know what, though?" Jill slid her sunglasses

down her nose and stared at me. "I think Tiimo likes you."

I felt two little spots of pink appear on my cheeks.

"I mean it, Gracie. I saw the way he kept looking at you last night, and you can't tell me that Murph and I didn't interrupt something."

I shrugged. "Who knows?"

"Listen, Gracie, Tiimo is neat. Really neat. He and I used to like each other in the sixth grade."

I smiled a little. Jill saw me and laughed again. "Oh yes. We were a very hot couple. Anyway, we've always been friends. He looks out for me, I look out for him."

Jill reached for the baby oil and rubbed some more on her shoulder. "Football tryouts start soon. Tiimo didn't make it last year, and he took it pretty hard. He's been working out ever since, trying to get ready for this year."

"Will he make it?"

"The coach is nuts if he doesn't put Tiimo on the roster. No one would work harder. But"—Jill bit her lower lip—"Tiimo isn't all that big. I'm as tall as he is." A helicopter taking off from one of the nearby hospitals beat the air like heavy wings, breaking the quiet of the afternoon.

Jill shrugged and the clouds left her face. "Oh well! I'm sure everything will work out just fine!"

Mom was standing on the front porch with Mrs. Burns when I got home. I could feel the muscles in my legs go tight, like I was getting ready to jump.

What was she doing here? Making trouble for Sinjian? Complaining to Mom?

As I got closer I could see that Mrs. Burns was holding Tatiana and Mom was actually petting her.

"Hi, Baby," she said in a voice that almost sounded like her own. "Isn't this the most beautiful cat you've ever seen?" She turned to Mrs. Burns. "Gracie used to feed the strays at home."

I started. I didn't realize that Mom had noticed.

Mrs. Burns looked at me like she couldn't believe I'd do such a thing. "It's a true sin the way most people take care of their pets," she said.

"I'm glad Tatiana has you," Mom said.

Mrs. Burns beamed.

"Talk to you again," Mom said as she went inside.

I followed and found her sitting on the couch, looking out the window, staring at nothing. The light in her eyes was gone again.

I shivered. Would I look like that someday, too?

"Hi, Baby. Where have you been—or did you tell me that already?" She frowned a little.

The telephone rang before I could answer her. Mom didn't move, so I picked up the receiver. It was someone with a question about Americalife.

"Just a minute, please," I said. "You better speak with my mom."

I handed the receiver to her, but she mouthed the words "not right now" to me.

I looked at her. She shook her head. I finally cradled the receiver to my ear.

"My mom's—busy. I'll have her call you back."

Did Jill's mother ever make her lie over the telephone for her?

I slammed the receiver down. "I hate doing that, you know," I said. "I really do."

"I'm sorry, Gracie," Mom said. She lay down on the couch and curled up into a ball. "I just don't feel very good." She tried to smile at me.

It used to be when she got like this that I'd run around our little house in American Fork trying to do anything to make her feel better—cover her with a blanket, take the phone off the hook, get her a diet Coke from the fridge. But I'd had it.

"Please, Mom. You need to do something—"

"I feel hollow, Gracie," she said like she hadn't heard me. "I'm an empty bucket. There's nothing inside of me."

"Get Pete to take you to the doctor!"

"There's no point. It's always going to be this way. Always." She turned her head and stared out the window again.

I put my hands together so they would stop shaking, and I swallowed hard.

"Okay," I said. "Fine. Don't go to the doctor. Don't take care of yourself. Don't do anything at all. Just sit here on the couch or on your bed all day long."

She didn't answer, just lifted a finger to twirl her hair. "I'm not going to cover for you," I said in a voice as quiet as stones. "I'm not going to lie for you anymore." Because *that's* what I hated most. The lies.

chapter 15

If you would have asked me the night before the parade how I felt, I might have said that things were looking up.

I could have sworn that Tiimo meant to kiss me that night in the park. But in the week that followed, he acted like nothing had happened. He came by the duplex with Murph—just like before, except he didn't talk as much as he used to. I didn't know what that meant.

I asked Jill about it one afternoon as we sipped diet Cherry Cokes at Hire's Drive-In.

"I still think he likes you," she said.

"He doesn't act like it."

"Maybe he's a little scared. Tiimo's never had a serious girlfriend before."

"Except for you in the sixth grade."

She laughed. "Right. Except for me in the sixth grade." She took another sip of her drink. "Gracie, I want to ask you something, but I don't want you to take offense, okay?"

I froze. Did she want to know something about our financial situation? Something about Mom?

"Have you *ever* thought about doing something—you know—different to your hair?"

I blinked. "Is there something wrong with it?" I suddenly felt sick inside, like I'd been making a fool of myself all along without realizing it until now.

"Oh no!" she said quickly. "In fact, you have *terrific* hair. I mean it. It's a great color and so thick, too. But I'm going to be real honest with you, okay? I like you a lot, Gracie. You're cute and smart, and I really want things to go well for you at school this year. Being new is tough — especially here—but you can make things easier on yourself if you look a little more like the other kids. Know what I mean?"

I nodded, embarrassed to the bone, afraid to open my mouth.

Jill reached out and lifted a lock of my hair. "This is how girls from small towns wear their hair," she said sadly.

"I *am* from a small town," I said in a small, cold voice.

Sudden tears filled Jill's soft brown eyes. "I didn't mean to hurt your feelings, Gracie. Honest."

I took a deep breath. I knew she was just trying to help. "It's okay."

Jill looked miserable. "My sister Kate's always telling me I have no tact, that I'm always saying stupid things."

151

"I like that about you."

She smiled a little. "That I say stupid things?"

I laughed. "No. That you say what you think. I like it when people are honest with me."

She reached across the table and squeezed my arm quickly. "I'm so glad you moved here," she whispered.

I took a long sip of Coke and avoided Jill's eyes. Was there something else I was doing wrong that I didn't know about?

I shivered.

Somebody like Jill had no idea what life was like for somebody like me. While I was worrying about whether or not our furniture was going to be repossessed, Jill was worrying about my hair.

Jill dropped me off in front of the duplex. As soon as I walked inside, I noticed how unnaturally dark everything was even though it was still early in the afternoon.

The shades. Someone had pulled every single one of them down.

"Mom?"

No answer.

Something was very wrong. I could feel my stomach start to roll.

"Mom!"

I walked quickly through the living room and past the kitchen where I noticed that the telephone receiver was off the hook and lying on the counter. The only thing Pete would get if he tried to call home was a busy signal.

I started to run.

Mom's bedroom door was shut tight. I threw it wide open and saw her lying stomach down on the bed. She was very still.

I screamed.

She didn't move at all as I rushed to her bed.

"Wake up, Mama! Please wake up!" I grabbed her by the shoulders and started to shake her hard. Strands of black hair flopped onto her face.

"I'm sorry I got mad at you," I yelled. "I'm sorry."

Stop it, Gracie. Stop it right now and think. Think!

The telephone. Run to the kitchen. Put the phone back on the hook. Now pick it up and punch out a number. 911.

The dispatcher's voice came through loud and clear.

Stop shaking. Stop.

"She's been depressed, and when I came home I found her on the bed—"

On the bed, still and white. My own mother.

"What's that? Yes. I'm pretty sure she's still breathing."

Address and phone number. My voice sounding so faraway, like hearing it on tape. Pete and Sinjian walking through the front door.

"Sinjian! Go to Tiimo's house. Right now!"

"I don't want to go."

"Get out of here!"

Pete watching me. Watching with round scared knowing eyes.

"Do what Gracie says. I'll pick you up later."

Words underwater. Everything sounding like it's underwater. Sinjian walking outside, Pete running into the bedroom.

"Oh God, Cynthia."

Sirens screaming like pain in my head. Outside. Ambulance, fire truck, squad cars.

"What's going on?" *Mrs. Burns standing on her porch holding her cat like a pillow.* "Is there a fire?"

"In there!" *Screaming to the paramedics who move in a dream.* "She's in there!"

"There's a fire in your house?" *Mrs. Burns's eyes frightened. People filling the street. Pain screaming like sirens through my head.*

Inside the house now, voices screaming through my head.

"The oxygen—"

"Move her here—"

"Careful—"

Pete moving like a puppy in the way.

"Cynthia, Cynthia. I love you—"

"Take her to Hope Medical Center—"

A woman in a uniform slipping her arms around my shoulders. "She's alive, honey. Your dad is going with us. How about you?"

"Jones! Nelson! Check the kid here."

"I'm fine."

Somebody giving me water, making me sit down on the couch.

"I'm fine."

"Take care of yourself. Take care."
Woman in blue whispering, whispering, whispering in my ear before taking Mommy away.

The phone rang, just like it had been ringing all afternoon. I knew it was Pete at the hospital, trying to let me know what was happening with Mom. I could see him in my mind, slipping into the hallway, sweating and breathing hard as he plunked a quarter in a pay phone, wondering why I didn't answer.

I didn't want to talk to him or anybody else.

My head . . .

I sat in the rocking chair, rocking back and forth, feeling cold and dead inside except for the hot white pain in my head.

Someone knocked at the front door.

I kept rocking.

Another knock. Then another. Now the person outside was pounding.

"Gracie!" It was Tiimo. "I know you're in there. I want to talk to you."

I got up slowly and opened the door.

The sunlight hurt my eyes. The pain in the right side of my head had turned into a knife. I looked at Tiimo, his hair shimmering like a halo of white fire. I felt sure he must be holding a flaming sword just like the Angel of Death. Coming for my mother. Coming for me.

"Can I come in?"

I pushed open the screen. He sat on the couch where he and Murph used to sit. Before.

"I'm sorry about your mother."

How much did he know? I laughed. Pain exploded like a firecracker behind my right eye.

"Are you okay, Gracie?"

"I'm fine." I spit the words out.

"Come home with me."

Out of the corner of my right eye, I saw little lights dancing like fireflies across the room. I was going to throw up.

Tiimo was rubbing his hands on his knees.

"I want you to leave now. Don't . . . ever come back." My words sounded far away and fuzzy, like they were floating through the air wrapped in cotton.

Maybe I could crawl to the couch, put a cushion over my head, curl up tight.

Tiimo left. "I'm sorry, Gracie," he said softly as he closed the door behind him.

I stumbled to the couch, groped for a pillow, collapsed, listened to the roar of the empty room.

chapter 16

~~~~~~~~~~~ ◆

Pete, his hair uncombed, looked tired and white when he came home from the hospital the next morning. He'd been there all night.

He put a piece of bread in the toaster and turned the control to dark.

"She's going to be fine, Gracie. Physically, anyway."

I didn't answer. I didn't do anything, even though the kitchen was a wreck. My headache went away sometime during the night, but every muscle in my body felt used up, just as though I'd spent the whole night running a race.

"How long will she be in the hospital?" I asked.

The toast popped up.

"As long as she needs to be," said Pete, slapping his toast carelessly with butter. He let out a long deep breath that left his chest looking like it had collapsed. "I told the doctor I didn't care how much it cost, I wanted Cynthia to stay until she was better. He then informed me that"—

Pete began to imitate the doctor in a flat whine—"Hope Medical Center has tax-exempt status and is therefore obligated to treat psychiatric patients regardless of their ability to pay!" A slow red flush crawled up his neck. "He was so cold, Gracie, standing there in his white coat acting like Cynthia—*Cynthia* of all people—was just another piece of white trash that had no business trying to kill herself if she couldn't afford it."

I had a mother who had tried to kill herself. I was that kind of girl.

"What should we tell Sinjian?" Pete asked.

"The truth." My voice sounded as cold and faraway as Alaska. "Tell him that his stepmother didn't care enough about any of us to stick around."

"Gracie!"

"Just tell him the truth. Kids want to know the truth. If he doesn't hear about it from us, he'll hear it from somebody else." I thought of the boys up the street who gave Sinjian a black eye. "Besides, he's probably already figured it out for himself."

Pete looked upset. "Do you really think so?"

"Kids aren't nearly as stupid as everybody wishes they were."

I could hear the old mantel clock ticking, filling the place with its cold and steady rhythm.

"I'll tell him later then," Pete said in a quiet voice that hardly sounded like his own. "I'll tell him the truth."

I looked like I didn't believe him, but Pete didn't notice. He went right on talking. "I've been thinking that I ought to find a steady job to tide us over until we can get Cynthia back on her feet. I've had some word-processing experience. Maybe I can find something around town."

I shivered and rubbed my arm. It was covered with goose bumps even though the new day was already warm.

"I'll get my Americalife business going later."

"What Americalife business? The whole thing has been a big joke, Pete, a big fat joke from first to last."

Pete looked at me, his eyes widening, his cheeks coloring, his mouth turning into an O.

"Maybe if you'd had a real job in the first place, none of this would have happened." I couldn't stop the words. "You should have done something, Pete. You should have made her go to the doctor. You knew. You *knew!*"

He lifted his head and stared straight at me.

Just then Sinjian flew into the kitchen. He was wearing an old bandana around his head and Pete's baggy black sweatshirt, even though it was getting hot outside. He pulled open a drawer and began rooting through it.

"I need a ninja weapon," he said. "Do we have something like—you know—a Chinese star?"

"A Chinese star?" Pete echoed.

Sinjian kept looking until he found a rusty old apple corer. "Aha! This is perfect!" Then he raced out of the kitchen and through the living room.

"Sinjian," Pete called after him, "I want to talk to you."

The front door banged shut.

* * *

Pete found a real job within the week. Just like that.

He put away his Americalife posters and got himself hired as a word processor in a big law office on Main Street. He goes to work every morning at eight and stops at the hospital every night on the way home.

Me, I haven't gone. Instead I sit on the couch and watch television. Just like my mother.

I was watching *All My Children* one morning when the room suddenly went dark. The sun had just passed behind a cloud.

Plink. Plink. Plink.

Sloppy raindrops began hitting the window outside. Erica Kane slunk like a small cat across the television screen, wearing a little black hat with a net veil and glossy pheasant feathers. So phony.

Plink. Plink.

The rain was coming down harder now, and I could smell the wet streets through the open window. I knew they would look as slick as a fish's back under the sky's gray light. This was the first time it had rained since we moved to Salt Lake City.

Plink.

Sinjian. Where was he? I'd been doing that lately. Losing track of Sinjian. Losing track of time. I sat up and listened for him outside.

"Well," pouted Erica, "I just don't understand why *everybody* is turning against me on this—"

I turned off the television, stepped out onto the front porch, and called Sinjian's name.

No answer.

"Sin-jian!"

Mrs. Burns poked her head out of the front door and opened her mouth to say something, but I didn't give her the chance.

I ran across the street, calling Sinjian's name.

The rain splashed hard against the sidewalk. I knew Sinjian didn't have his jacket. Also, he was probably doing something dangerous like standing underneath big trees so that he wouldn't get struck by lightning.

I went back into the house, slipped a hooded sweatshirt on, and found an umbrella that had two of the spokes missing. Then I went to look for Sinjian.

I slogged through the alley where Sinjian usually played ninjas by himself. There was no sign of him.

"Sinjian!"

The air overhead was filled with the hollow cooing of pigeons huddling in house eaves. A wet dog with his nose in an overturned garbage can started and ran away at the sound of my voice, leaving behind an empty tuna can, a soggy paper bag from Hire's Drive-In, and a plastic pot with dried-up flowers. I remembered the potted flowers Sinjian brought home the night of Pete's Americalife meeting. Could he be at the cemetery right now?

I walked up O Street

The wet sky and heavy branches of ancient spruce trees made a gloomy canopy over the cemetery. Old tombstones, most of them carved out of red rock, stood at crazy angles from each other.

I shivered.

"Sin-jian! Sin-jian!"

I half-expected to hear my own echo in that place, but the sound of my voice was swallowed by the moist dense air around me.

"Sin-jian!"

No answer. Just the noise of rain on my umbrella, on trees, on grass.

The tombstones were covered with carved symbols like sheaves of wheat or hands without arms pointing upward. The names of people were etched below.

> Clarissa Ann Church
> b. Gloucestershire, England, 1839
> d. Salt Lake City, 1856
> Heaven hath called our dear Sister Home.

I reached out, touched the tombstone, traced the words that the wind hadn't swept away yet with my finger.

Suddenly there was a picture in my mind—Mom lying on her bed. Eyes closed. Mouth barely breathing. Me screaming.

It was always the same picture. Whenever I shut my eyes at night or looked away from the TV or stared out the window, it was there waiting for me.

How *long* would I have to remember?

A noise.

Sinjian leaped out from behind a tree about fifty yards

away from me. He had the same old bandana wrapped around his head, and he held a long stick. He didn't know I was there.

Sinjian did a jump kick, then started swinging the stick in circles with one hand high over his head, just like it was a helicopter propeller.

Crack! He brought the stick down hard on top of a tombstone. *Crack! Crack!* He twirled down the aisle of markers, hitting them all with his stick as he went. Anger twisted his face.

I started to shake.

Crack!

I opened my mouth to call Sinjian, but nothing came out. He moved farther away, leaping and swinging his stick and chanting the words to a song I couldn't hear until I could barely see him.

I turned and ran away, praying he didn't see me.

At home I went straight to my room and peeled off all my wet clothes, letting them fall from my hand with a little plop to the floor, until I was completely naked. Then I crawled between the sheets and curled my knees up tight to my chest.

I called Sarah that evening.

"Were you serious when you told me I could live with you?" I asked.

She squealed into my ear. "Yes!"

"Your parents really won't care?"

"Are you kidding? They think you're a Good Influence on me."

"Where will I sleep?"

Sarah let out an exasperated sigh. "Will you *please* stop acting like a person's mother? You can sleep in Rachel and Rebecca's bed. I'll drown them before you get here."

After I hung up the telephone, I went to the coat closet and dragged a suitcase from a top shelf. It was heavy. When I opened it, I found that it was still full of Pete's old books. I dumped them out. These were absolutely the last things of his I was going to unpack.

The books were mostly paperbacks, old and yellow, some of them held together with wide red rubber bands. Pete liked science fiction mostly—Piers Anthony, Isaac Asimov, Frank Herbert—which figured. Make-believe. Pretend. Fake.

I picked up one book that was different from the others—larger and a little heavier. It was called *Shyness: What It Is and How to Overcome It.*

Holding that book gave me a funny feeling inside, like I'd looked deep into his drawer at something private that he didn't want anybody to see.

"Gracie?"

I dropped the book quickly and turned around. Pete was standing in the doorway. He held his suit coat in one hand, a cheap imitation leather briefcase in the other. His top button was undone and his tie was loose. His face was flushed from the heat.

"What are you doing, Gracie?" he asked quietly.

"I'm emptying this stupid suitcase."

Pete didn't move. "Are you going somewhere?"

"Yes."

There was a long pause. "Can I ask where?"

"I'm going to live with Sarah. I'm leaving this afternoon."

Pete shifted his weight, then ran his fingers through his hair. Lines appeared on his sweaty forehead.

"Please, don't leave. Please—" He took a step toward me and I pulled back.

Pete stopped, then took a loud deep breath. "Will you do me one favor, please. Cynthia asks about you. Will you stop at the hospital to say good-bye?"

"She didn't try to say good-bye to me."

Pete looked straight at me with sad eyes. "Gracie, Gracie—"

"Leave me alone."

"Don't worry about the books. I'll take care of them."

I'll take care of them. Where had I heard that before? Another pause.

"What do you want me to tell Sinjian?" Pete asked.

My hands started to shake as I stacked one book on top of another. I didn't want to be here when Sinjian found out.

"Tell him anything you want. I don't care."

I don't care!

165

chapter 17

As I looked around the bus at the people traveling with me—the old lady with no teeth sipping a Big Gulp, a clean-cut kid who probably went to Brigham Young University in Provo, a middle-aged couple speaking to each other in German—I thought of another difference between me and Jill. Jill never rides the bus. Once when I suggested we ride the bus downtown, she looked at me in surprise.

"The bus?"

I nodded.

"But Kate can drive us to the mall, Gracie. I promise she won't mind. Besides, I wouldn't even know which bus to catch."

When I told her it wasn't that hard to figure out—here's the funny part—she looked at me with real respect.

The heat outside made mirages in the middle of the street that looked like distant puddles of oily water. It was hot inside the bus, too, hot and stuffy even though the air conditioning was on. I wanted fresh air to blow through an open window and sweep away the smells of stale smoke, stale sweat.

The old lady started to talk to me. "I'll bet he thinks all the pretty girls love him," she said in a sing-song voice, pointing at the clean-cut boy. Then she cackled. The boy gave her a polite but distant smile, the kind nice people always give when they finally realize they're dealing with a crazy person.

I looked out the window.

The bus lumbered over a viaduct, out of the city and into the flat burnt valley surrounded by hard purple mountains. I would like a heart like this valley, I thought, a heart ringed with stone.

Sarah was waiting for me at the bus stop.

"You look great," she said when she saw me. "Have you been losing weight or something?"

"I don't know," I said. "I haven't been trying to." Just like Mom.

Sarah was full of things to tell me. "They painted your old house," she said. "The family who moved in there painted it yellow. *Yellow* if you can even believe it."

Everything is changing, I thought as we walked to Sarah's house.

Two of Sarah's little sisters, Rachel and Rebecca, were sitting in the middle of Sarah's bedroom floor making their Barbies talk to each other.

"Let's go to the beach now, okay?"

"Okay! I'll call our boyfriends."

Sarah screamed. "I told you stupid kids that this is mine and Gracie's bedroom now. Get out of here!"

"Let's wear our new bikinis, okay?"

"Okay!"

Sarah stomped over to Rachel. She grabbed the Barbie and threw it into the hall. Rachel started to cry, and I winced.

"I'm telling Mom," Rebecca screamed.

"Shut up," said Sarah.

"They can stay here, Sarah," I said, wanting to hold Rachel in my arms. "Come on."

Sarah picked up fistfuls of Barbie clothes and threw them out of the room.

"You'll lose all the shoes!" Rebecca was crying, too.

"Where are they going to sleep? Huh?" My voice was climbing. "Did you think about that, Sarah?"

"I'm sick of these guys!" Sarah was still chucking things. "They're always in my face."

"Just stop it!" I was yelling now. "Stop treating them like that!"

"Who do you think you are?" Sarah turned on me. "My mother?"

We glared at each other while Rebecca and Rachel huddled their blond heads together like little white rabbits. I finally turned to them. "It's okay, you guys. I'll sleep on the floor."

Sarah swore at me as I walked out of the room.

*   *   *

We watched a baseball game on TV with Sarah's brothers Josh, Danny, Luke, and Matthew. Although watching baseball is about the most boring thing in the world to do, it was certainly better than having a conversation with Sarah.

Was Sarah always so mean to her family?

"I'm s-o-o-o-o-o bored, Gracie," she finally said. "Let's go for a walk."

"Hey, do us a favor," said Luke. "Don't come back."

Sarah picked up a couch pillow and threw it straight at his head, only she hit the television and knocked a pile of *National Geographics* off it instead.

"You throw like a girl," said Luke.

It was still warm outside even though it was dark.

"I hate Luke," Sarah moaned. "I also hate hot weather. Where do you want to go?"

I shrugged.

"Let's walk down the tracks," she said.

"Fine."

We walked along, stepping over loose gravel and onto the ties like a couple of kids trying to miss the cracks in a sidewalk. Sarah started to sing. "I love him just like a whatever—whatever—"

"Why don't you ever take the time to actually learn the words to a song?"

"Well, please excuse me for breathing the same air as you," said Sarah.

What was wrong with me?

"You've been in a really lousy mood ever since you got here, Gracie, and I'm getting real sick of it."

"I'm sorry," I said. "Ignore me, okay?"

"Is it that time of the month or something?"

"Yeah," I lied. "It is."

Sarah laughed. "Remember when we were in junior high school how worried we used to get that our periods would start in the middle of class and that all the boys would know?"

I kicked a stone loose and watched it skip ahead of me. Did I ever care about something like that?

Sarah stopped. "Listen."

There was a train rumbling in the distance.

"I can't believe it," she said. "Mom always has a fit about us kids walking on the tracks but this is the first I ever remember a train coming."

I laughed.

"We better get off," said Sarah.

I kept on walking.

"Gracie?"

The train was getting closer. I could feel vibrations moving up from the tracks through the soles of my shoes.

Sarah caught up with me and grabbed my arm. "Let's go!"

I shook her off.

"There's a train coming. A *train!*"

"So?"

It was in sight now, turning the bend like a big metal animal.

"What is the matter with you? Are you crazy?" Sarah's eyes were huge.

"Sure. What did you expect?"

The train whistled. Goose bumps chased down my arms.

"Holy shit!" Sarah leaped off the tracks.

I walked straight ahead.

"Gracie!"

An old jump rope rhyme started beating through my head in time with the clackety-clack of the wheels.

—one, two, three, four, five, six, seven—

The noise filled my whole body.

—all good children go to heaven—

My hair flew up from my ears. I chanted the rhyme out loud.

"—five, six, seven—"

Light was shining on my face, making me blind. Heat rose up around my legs.

"—all good children go to—"

I stepped off the track.

"I hate you!" I screamed. *"I hate you—"*

The engine roared past, scattering my words to the sky.

Clackety-clackety-clack

"Gracie?" Sarah was on the other side of the tracks. She looked both ways just like a little kid crossing the street, then stepped over the tracks to me.

My ears were ringing.

"Gracie?"

We stared at each other.

"You scared me to death! What the hell were you *doing?*"

I didn't answer.

"That was the stupidest thing I have *ever* seen anybody do in my entire life." She shook me by the shoulders. "You could have been killed. Is that what you wanted?"

I started shivering so hard my teeth chattered.

"No," I said in a small voice. "That's not what I want"

"Oh, Gracie!" Sarah hugged me and started to cry. "Gracie, Gracie. Don't ever do that again. You scared me so bad." She gulped. "I'd die if something happened to you."

I wrapped my arms around her. "I'm okay, Sarah. I promise I am."

She pulled away from me and searched my face. "Let's go home. Right now."

"I don't want to go back yet. I want to be by myself." I gave her a weak smile.

"I think you should go home with me."

I laughed a little. "I'm okay. Really."

Sarah was still staring at me hard.

"I just want to walk around for a while," I said. "Think some things through. I'll be careful. You don't have to worry about me."

Sarah gave me one last squeeze. "And everybody thinks I'm the wild one," she whispered.

*   *   *

I walked.

I walked and walked and walked—past the tabernacle and City Hall and the park on Main Street where they hold the carnival during Steel Days. I walked past the little hospital and the cemetery where Sarah and I once dared each other to jump into an open grave. It was like taking a walk through my life. I walked until I finally ended up at the place where I wanted to be all along.

Our old house. Mine and Mom's.

Sarah was right—it was yellow now, not blue, and there was a new wreath made out of grapevines hanging on the door. Yellow and orange marigolds were growing in the front yard.

You could tell the people living there now loved the house. I was happy for that.

I heard someone singing through an open window. I caught my breath, then stepped from the street onto the grass.

It was a deep, throaty woman's voice.

I moved closer to the window, holding my breath, hoping nobody would see me.

It was a whiskey voice like Mom's.

"—you'll come to me when the day is done—"

Closer and closer. I crept up to the window, then dropped to the ground so that the shadows would slip over me.

"—when night has dimmed the setting sun—"

I crouched there, listening to her sing, just like I was a

little girl again waking up from a bad dream and needing her to make me feel safe again.

The radio announcer's voice crackled through the window. "It's eighty-two degrees in the City of Salt tonight—"

I started to cry. For the very first time since Mom went away. I cried and cried like I would never stop.

I just missed her so much.

The sun was pouring through the window and shining straight on to my face, but that wasn't what woke me up the next morning. My dream did.

I dreamed that Sinjian was only two or three inches long, and that I put him in my top drawer with enough bird seed and water to last him until I got back to Salt Lake. Only when I returned I discovered that he'd turned blue because he couldn't breathe.

My eyes flew open.

Everybody was downstairs eating breakfast. When I walked into the kitchen, they all stopped talking. Just like that. The little kids stared. The older ones pretended they hadn't seen me. Only Baby Zach, dumping mush on his head, smiled and squealed.

Sarah had told them about last night.

"Morning, Gracie," said Mr. Macleod, giving me a sad little smile. He was all dressed and ready for another day at Geneva.

I swallowed and nodded. I couldn't *believe* that Sarah had told them.

"What can I get you to eat, Honey?" Mrs. Macleod asked.

"Cereal. Cereal would be great. Thanks."

Josh and Danny scooted over and made room for me at the end of the bench. Sarah sat across from me, looking guilty.

It was pretty funny, I thought, the way Sarah was always saying how much she hated her family. But when it came right down to it, she could talk to them.

Suddenly I felt lonelier than I'd ever felt in my whole life.

Mrs. Macleod gave me a plastic bowl filled with hot oatmeal.

What was Sinjian eating for breakfast?

I could feel Josh looking at me out of the corner of his eye. Everybody was watching to see what I would do next. I flushed as I cleared my throat.

"Are you playing baseball again this summer, Josh?" Good. My voice sounded even.

He nodded, his cheeks puffed out with cereal.

"So are you guys any good?"

"They got their butts whipped yesterday," piped up Danny. "Josh was pitching."

Josh shoved Danny and all the little kids laughed.

"He throws like a girl," said Sarah.

"Quit it," said Mr. Macleod. "All of you."

But it was too late. Everybody was talking and laughing and teasing at the same time.

I breathed a sigh of relief.

175

"You girls got something fun planned today?" Mrs. Macleod asked, putting a piece of buttered toast in front of me.

I said something that surprised even myself. "I'm going back to Salt Lake."

"What?" Sarah shouted over the noise. "You're going back to Salt Lake? You just got here!"

"I have to go back, Sarah. I'm sorry."

"You're mad at me," she said. "I know you are."

"I'm not. I have to go back. I want to go back."

"Why?"

I shrugged helplessly. Who knew?

Mrs. Macleod put her hand on my shoulder and gave it a squeeze.

The place was empty when I got home. I hoped Pete had made arrangements for Sinjian before he went to work that morning.

The phone rang.

It was Jill. "Gracie!"

The day after Mom tried to commit suicide, Jill had called and told me how sorry she was. Since then she'd worked very hard to act normal around me, like nothing unusual had happened. Sometimes she dropped by with diet Cokes or magazines, but mostly she called, trying to get me to do something—anything—with her.

"Hi," I said.

"I'm having a party Friday night. Promise you'll come. *Promise!"*

"I don't know—"

"Tiimo will be there."

Which was an even better reason not to go. Whenever I thought about the last time Tiimo and I saw each other, my insides withered.

"Great," I said.

"I'm counting on you, Gracie," Jill said as she hung up.

The phone rang again a few minutes later. I didn't recognize the caller's voice.

"May I speak to Sinjian Wilding's parent, please?"

My heart started to beat just a little faster. "They're not home right now, but I'm his . . . sister. Can I help you?"

"Look, this is Max at Western Garden. I found this little guy here trying to pocket something that doesn't belong to him." He almost sounded apologetic. "Can you get somebody down here to help me straighten this out?"

I swallowed hard. "Yes. We'll be over right away."

"Fine. Just ask for Max. We'll be waiting in the back office."

My hand was shaking as I hung up the phone. What should I do? I could take the bus, get Sinjian myself.

My heart started to pound even faster.

The truth was that I did not want to talk to the man who was waiting with Sinjian in the back office. I picked up the phone and punched out the number of the law firm where Pete worked.

When he answered, I was breathing hard. "I need your help."

There was a pause. "Gracie? Where are you?"

"I'm at home. Sinjian's in trouble. I just got a call from some man at Western Garden who said he caught Sinjian shoplifting."

"Ulla couldn't watch him today so I left him with someone I sold Americalife to." Pete swore, and I felt a stab of guilt. I should have been watching him.

"Hang on," Pete said. "I'll be right home."

I waited on the front porch. What did Sinjian try to steal? Did the police know? Would he have to go to the police station so they could question him?

Pete pulled up in front of the curb and honked. I ran to the pickup and crawled inside.

"What the hell was that kid thinking?" Pete spluttered. His face was bright red, and he was spraying spit all over the steering wheel. "What does a kid steal at Western Garden, for hellsake. Tulips?"

"That's where he buys birdseed."

"Do you think Sinjian was stealing birdseed?!"

My stomach was churning, turning upside down. If Max at Western Garden didn't make life miserable for Sinjian, then Pete definitely would.

"What the hell . . ." Pete kept saying.

Sinjian and Max were waiting for us in the back office. Max, a tall lean man with silver hair, stood up from behind a metal desk when Pete and I walked through the door.

"I'm Peter Wilding," said Pete, stretching out a hand for Max to shake. "Sinjian's dad."

178

Max smiled a little as he ran a thick hand through his hair. "I found Sinjian here trying to take this." He dug into a pocket of his plaid workshirt and fished out—a dog collar. It was the kind that looks like a small chain. The collar dangled from Max's hand. Sinjian was staring at his shoes, his cheeks flushed brown and red.

"I'm really very sorry about this," Pete was saying, still looking at the dog collar like he couldn't believe what he was seeing. "He knows better. Don't you, Sinjian."

Sinjian's head bobbed straight up. "Yessir," he mumbled.

"What do you say?" Pete prompted. Even though his voice sounded fairly calm, I could see a neck vein standing out like a thick piece of twine.

"I'm sorry," said Sinjian.

Max sat down on the edge of his desk and looked straight at Sinjian. "I didn't call the police, but I want you to understand what a serious offense it is to take something that doesn't belong to you."

Sinjian nodded miserably.

"If you want something you see in a store, what should you do?"

"Buy it," said Sinjian.

Max pocketed the collar. "Okay then. Let's not let something like this happen again."

"Thank you," said Pete. "Thank you for being so—understanding."

He shook Max's hand, then walked over to Sinjian.

"We're going home now," said Pete in an icy voice.

Max shot Sinjian a sympathetic look as the three of us walked out of the office.

Pete yelled all the way home while Sinjian sat between us, his chin buried in his chest.

"I didn't bring you up to take things that don't belong to you! You know better than that!"

"But I wasn't going to steal it! I put it in my pocket while I looked at the birds and then I just forgot about it."

"A choke chain? We don't even have a dog for crying out loud!" said Pete.

"I thought it was a ninja weapon," Sinjian mumbled.

Pete and I looked at each other.

"A *what?*" Pete exploded.

"I thought it was a ninja weapon!" Sinjian yelled.

"I don't care if you thought it was a nuclear warhead. You don't take things that aren't yours. Got that?!"

"Will everybody please stop screaming at each other?" I was screaming myself.

Sinjian hunched down further and Pete stared angrily out the windshield.

Pete told Sinjian to go to his room when we got home. "And don't come out until I say you can."

Sinjian ran to the room and slammed the door behind him. Pete let out a heavy sigh, then sank onto the couch. I sat down in the rocking chair.

"What am I going to do, what am I going to do?" Pete turned his head to look out the window.

He didn't sound like he was feeling sorry for himself.

180

He didn't even sound mad anymore. He just sounded tired. When I looked at him, I felt a new little pain growing in my chest.

"I've always been way too hard on Sinjian," Pete said without looking at me. "No one needs to tell me that. Even when he was just a little boy I'd yell at him more than I should because I thought he wasn't doing things as well as other kids his age. I'd yell at him and then watch that poor kid wilt right in front of me, and I'd hate myself for the way I was treating him. So what did I do? Jump all over him again the very next time something happened." Pete paused. "It's just when I look at him sometimes I think of all the stupid things I used to do—that I still do—and I don't want him to be like me. I hope to God he doesn't turn out like me."

The hurt in my heart was still growing.

"Sometimes," I heard myself say, "sometimes Sinjian reminds me of myself when I was a kid, too. There were times when I was . . . kind of unhappy."

Pete slowly shifted his gaze from the window to my face. We looked at each other for a very long time. "I'm sure that's true," he said softly.

I twisted my hands into a tight knot.

"Lily called Sinjian last night."

"Oh, I'm so glad. A kid always wants to know—" I stopped. "*Why* did she call, Pete? After all this time."

"I got in touch with her and told her she had to write or call at least once a week. She apologized and said the summer had gotten away from her because she's stopped

181

thinking of time in linear terms. Whatever that means." He laughed a little.

I looked at Pete. "Thank you," I whispered.

"No, Gracie. Thank you."

I looked at him for a moment. "It isn't your fault!"

"Are you talking about your mom?"

I nodded. Pete stared at his shoes, and I felt my throat go tight.

"It isn't," I said.

"But I do blame myself. Remember that time when I told you to fix her something to eat, then I left in a hurry? I knew you were going to ask me for help. But I didn't want to hear you say the words. I wanted to believe that Cynthia was okay, that I was enough to make her happy." Pete's voice stayed the same, but his eyes were wet. "Of all the stupid things I've done in my life, that was the worst."

"I think it was mean of her to do what she did," I heard myself say. "I think it was the meanest thing I've ever heard of."

Pete quickly wiped his eyes with the back of his hand and looked at me straight. "You *know* if your mother was feeling like herself she wouldn't have swallowed those pills."

"I hate her." Each word came clear and hard from my mouth.

Pete didn't tell me to be quiet or contradict me. He just looked at me instead with sad eyes. Then he started rubbing his forehead like he had a bad headache.

"You know, Gracie, sometimes I think everybody in this family is a little bit nuts. Me. Cynthia. Sinjian. We all need shrinks. Everybody except for you. You're the sanest person I ever met. Tough, too. You take things straight on, and you don't back down from a fight. I know *that* from personal experience. Your mother is so sweet, but I'm afraid—I'm so afraid she doesn't know how to fight."

Without even knowing it, Pete had found my secret.

"Do I remind you very much of my mother?" I asked him in a tiny voice.

Pete stopped rubbing his forehead and blinked. Then he actually smiled. "You? Well you *look* just like her. But no. You're not like her *at all*."

"But do you—do you think I will be when I'm her age?" My heart was racing. I had to know.

He laughed right out loud. "Are you serious?"

"But we like the same things . . ." I persisted.

"Right. Like me, for instance."

I had to smile, too.

Pete went on talking. "Wanna hear something dumb? I've been real scared of you, Gracie. You're just so competent. Do you realize that if it weren't for you we'd probably all have starved to death?"

I thought of the boxes of Americalife pills and powders stacked against his bedroom wall. But I didn't say anything.

Outside I could hear summer evening noises—kids playing kick the can, crickets, sprinklers, a radio somewhere.

183

"You know you're pretty amazing, Gracie." He stopped. "Hey! That's what I'll call you from now on. Amazing Gracie!"

Usually I hate how corny Pete's jokes are. They sound like they come straight out of the joke books you find sitting on the shelves of a grade school library.

I smiled.

Pete started to laugh his wheezy laugh. "Oh geez—"

"What's so funny?"

"Well, it isn't really funny I guess . . ." He laughed some more.

"Tell me!"

"Sinjian. Getting busted for stealing a dog collar."

"Not a dog collar," I corrected. "A ninja weapon."

We looked at each other, then burst out laughing. Pete's shoulders were shaking.

"That kid. What an imagination, huh?"

"He's got a *great* imagination," I agreed.

The sound of a distant fire engine racing toward somewhere in the valley drifted through an open window.

"I'm so glad you came home," said Pete.

I went for a walk after that. The box elder trees lining the street caught the late afternoon sun with their tattered leafy branches, then spilled shadows on the sidewalk below. Normally I would have thought about how ugly box elder trees are and how much I missed the fruit trees in American Fork. But this time I hardly noticed them because of the words playing through my head.

You're not like her at all.

Pete's words made me feel as free as wind.

Suddenly, something bright and yellow at the side of the street caught my eye. I stopped and looked again.

Sunflowers! There were sunflowers growing in just a little crack of dirt between the gutter and the street.

I smiled to myself.

I could tell Sinjian was still awake even though he was pretending to be asleep when I went to bed that night. His eyelids were scrunched closed so tight that they fluttered. Kids don't seem to realize that nobody looks like that when they're really asleep.

"Sinjian?"

No answer.

"I know you're faking."

He still didn't move, so I sat down on the edge of his bed. "Okay, then, I'm going to tell Sinjian-who-is-sleeping something I just recently realized. I realized that I like the way he eats a whole box of cereal in one day so that he can get to the prize. I like the way he sings me silly songs and the way he combs his hair straight up and the way he wears just one glove and also the way he can make people blind in one eye. I like the way he always wants to sit at the back of the bus and tell me lies about dinosaurs, and I really like how soft his face looks when he pets Dr. Seuss."

I could see the moon shine like a pearl through the

window above his head. I used to *just* love the way the moon looked when Mom sang songs to me.

"I hate Dad," he said into his pillow.

"Yeah. Well. It probably feels like that to you."

Sinjian sat up and curled up like a cat into a tight little ball.

"You're always mad at me, too. Everybody's always mad at me."

Normally I would have said something like, "That's because you do things that make people angry." But tonight I didn't say anything.

Here's the thing I'm finally figuring out all over again about little kids. They say things they don't mean because they don't know how to say what they really want to. A kid who says he hates his parents probably doesn't really hate them. He just may be frustrated or tired or mad. Or hurt.

I ran my fingers through the top of Sinjian's hair. It needed washing bad.

"Hey, you know what? I think things are going to be fine," I said. "Your dad and me—we're going to help you. Okay?"

His arms were suddenly around my waist, tight as a belt, and his face was buried in my side.

"I love you, Sinjian."

He didn't answer, didn't make any noise at all, which is unusual for Sinjian.

But I could tell he was crying just the same.

chapter 18

I looked at Mrs. Lehtinen's fern on top of the bookshelf.

No doubt about it. It was making a comeback, just like one of those former child stars you're always reading about in *TV Guide*. Lately I'd been mixing a little Americalife powder into its water, and I'd been getting pretty amazing results.

The telephone rang, and I froze.

It was Friday—the day of the big party. Somehow I'd have to tell Jill that I wasn't coming.

"Hello."

"It's Murph."

"Oh." I certainly hadn't expected a call from Murph.

"You still there?" Murph asked. "You haven't croaked or nothin' since you picked up the phone?"

"I'm still here."

"I'm real worried about Tiimo right now," said Murph, getting straight to the point. "Things aren't going so terrific for him right now, and I'm calling to let you know that you haven't been such a swell pal lately."

I could feel my face start to burn. Who did Murph think he was?

"Well, to tell you the truth," I said as coolly as I could, "things haven't been going so good for me either."

"Yeah, I heard. Everybody knows your mom tried to o.d."

I almost stopped breathing.

"Go to hell," I whispered. I started to hang up the phone, but I heard Murph yell, "I'm sorry, Gracie. I'm sorry. That was a stupid thing to say."

"You're right. It was really stupid."

There was a long pause on the other end of the line. "Look, I just wanted to let you know that Tiimo found out yesterday that he didn't make the football team. It may not sound like a big deal to you right now, but—I guess I thought you oughta know. He's taking it bad."

"Thanks for telling me," I said slowly. Then I remembered that Murph had tried out, too. "What about you? Did you make the team?"

"Oh yeah," said Murph, and he almost sounded angry. "I made it just fine."

"Well. Congratulations."

"I guess." Murph hung up.

I put the receiver back on its cradle thoughtfully. So Tiimo didn't make the team. Even though he'd worked out all summer. Even though he'd given everything he had during practices. Even though he'd believed more than anything else in the world that it was possible.

I remembered his face the night before the parade, how fierce it was, but how full of hope, too. How did his face look when he found out he'd been cut? Was he standing around the gym door, looking for his name on a list with a bunch of other guys? Maybe he read it three or four times, just to be sure. What did he say when he realized that his name wasn't there?

I picked up the phone again and dialed Jill's number.

"Look," I said after we said hello, "I just found out about Tiimo."

"Can you believe it? I'd love to kill that stupid coach."

"Do you think he'll be at your house tonight?"

"Murph is bringing him whether he wants to come or not. It will be hard for him, though. A lot of his friends who made the team will be here."

I thought about this.

"You're coming aren't you, Gracie? You promised."

"Yeah," I said slowly. "I'll be there. I'm not sure how thrilled Tiimo will be." I gave a light laugh like I didn't care anyway.

"Oh *right.*"

"I haven't seen him for a while."

"You told him to stay away."

"I—I guess I didn't really mean it."

Jill let out a mighty snort of contempt. "Guys are so incredibly stupid. They never know what you really mean."

I thought about this, too.

"See you tonight, Jill," I finally said.

"You can't back out on me now" were her final words.

When I hung up the phone I realized that this was the first time in a long time that I'd thought about somebody else's problems besides my own family's.

I took one look at myself in the bathroom mirror after talking to Jill and decided I needed to do something with my hair. Immediately.

I found an old issue of *Seventeen* magazine that Jill loaned me and thumbed through it for ideas. The girls were all tall and leggy. Nobody looked like me although a few of them did look like Jill. I remembered what she'd said that day at Hire's Drive-In about changing my hair style. I found a picture of a girl with Jill's hair and ripped it out of the magazine.

An hour later I was waiting for my turn at Foxy Freddy's, which is the kind of place with a sign in the window that says WE WELCOME WALK-INS! The inside looked a little like a McDonald's, only there were mirrors and swivel chairs instead of booths and tables. A Muzak melody competed with the noisy hum of blow-dryers, and the air was thick with the fumes of permanent waves.

This definitely wasn't the kind of place Jill's mom took her. Jill once told me that they served customers wine and cheese at the salon she went to. I looked at her like she was crazy and said I preferred to keep the experiences of eating and having my hair cut separate.

"Next?"

A huge man with cowboy boots and long blond hair stood before me, holding a plastic cape.

I blinked.

"I think you're next," he said. He offered me his hand, then pulled me to my feet.

"This way. We'll wash your hair first."

I followed him through a crowd of women clipping hair and took a chair in front of a sink. He secured the plastic cape around my neck, twirled me around, let down the back of the chair, and told me to put my head back.

"Relax," he said. "I've got great hands."

The steady sound of spraying water next to my ear was almost as soothing as the feel of it on my scalp.

"I *hate* this music," the man washing my hair said. "It sounds like funeral music. Do you like funeral music?" Then he shouted over the other noises. "Hey, who ordered the funeral music? By the way," he said to me in a normal voice again, "my name is Kyp and you are—"

"Gracie."

"Gracie. *Fabulous* name. Over here."

Kyp led me to his station and dropped his voice way down low as he pumped my chair up with his foot.

"You're very lucky I got to you before someone else did. Nearly everybody else who works here is scissor-happy. Real cliptomaniacs, if you know what I mean."

I nodded weakly.

He flashed a white smile at me. "So what did you have in mind?"

I pulled the magazine picture from my purse. "Something like this, maybe." But suddenly I wasn't so sure.

Kyp took the picture from my hand and studied it carefully.

"Bangs, too?"

"I guess so . . ." My voice was starting to shrink, just like Alice in Wonderland.

I looked in the mirror at my soaking wet hair, flat and black against my head. What would *I* look like with Jill's hair?

"This is a hot cut right now," Kyp was saying. "Very hot. I must have done this cut three times already this morning on girls just your age."

So not only would I look like Jill, but I would look just like everybody else around here, too. Was that what I really wanted?

Sarah was always changing her hair—the style, the cut, the color. Whenever he wanted to make her mad, Sarah's brother Joseph said she changed her hair more often than she changed her underwear.

Kyp reached for his scissors and lifted a strand of my hair.

Well, I wasn't Sarah. Or Jill.

"I think—I think I'll wait for a while," I said. "Can you just shape my hair a little so it won't look so shaggy? It's been falling in my face a lot lately."

192

Kyp grinned.

When he finished trimming and styling my hair, Kyp gave me a hand mirror so I could see it from every angle.

It looked just like me.

"You're beautiful, Gracie," he whispered. *"Gorgeous!"*

When I stood on Jill's porch I could hear music and laughter, and even though it was barely dusk, the whole house streamed with ribbons of electric light. It had been so long since I'd seen anybody but Jill. What would people do when they saw me? What would they say? I shivered.

Jill answered the door. "Gracie!" She threw her arms around me. "I'm so glad you came!"

She led me inside to the kitchen first, where her mom and little sister were busy making mini-pizzas out of English muffins.

"Look who's here!" Jill announced.

Mrs. Tanner smiled. "Oh, Gracie, it's *so* good to see you."

I held my breath, waiting to see if she would mention my mother. She didn't. I felt my shoulders relax.

"Can I help or anything?" I asked.

Mrs. Tanner laughed. "Do you know that you are the only teenager in the entire universe that has *ever* asked me that question?"

Jill pulled a face at her mother, and Mrs. Tanner laughed again.

"No, you definitely may not help me, Gracie. Go downstairs and have some fun. That's an order."

The family room downstairs was packed with kids. A few of the girls were shooting pool while some boys looked on. Another group was huddled around the television, playing a Nintendo game. The rest were spread on the floor and couch and chairs, talking and laughing. Murph was throwing popcorn at people's heads.

Watching them, I suddenly realized that life had gone on for everybody else. The fact that my mother had swallowed pills was old news by now, probably not even very interesting.

Tiimo. Where was he? I scanned the room, but when I finally saw him, my stomach sank straight to my knees.

He was in a corner of the room talking to another girl. He was smiling, she was laughing. Suddenly, the whole room felt hot. I wanted to be outside where I could breathe fresh air. Alone.

So why shouldn't he talk to another girl? I asked myself as I walked back upstairs. *Stop acting like this.* But I kept right on going.

I sat down in a cast-iron love seat on the front porch. A breeze from a distant canyon cooled my flaming cheeks. I folded my hands into a tight little ball to keep them from trembling.

You told him to get lost. What did you expect?

I couldn't go home yet. Jill would notice. I would just sit here for a while.

"Gracie?"

I jumped at the sound of Tiimo's voice.

"Oh," I said casually. "Hi." I was glad that it was dark enough to hide my blush.

"I saw you leave. I hoped you weren't going home."

"Not yet," I said lightly. "I just wanted a little fresh air." Did people say things like that to each other in real life?

Tiimo took the white chair across from me. Neither of us said anything for a minute.

"Did I tell you that my mom finally broke down and bought herself a car?" he asked. "All these years in America and she's never owned a car. Mummi thinks we're all going to be killed."

I laughed. "Well, you know how grandmothers are." Actually, I don't remember either one of my grandmothers.

Tiimo's eyes caught mine, and I saw the sadness there.

"Murph called me, you know. He told me that you didn't make the team."

Tiimo let out a short laugh. "Did he also tell you what the coach said to me?"

I shook my head.

"He said I was too small to play football but that he'd really love me to be the team manager. Like that's supposed to make me feel better."

"You don't want to be a manager?" I wasn't even sure what a team manager did.

"I want to *play* football, Gracie, not stand on the sidelines and pass out little drinks of water to the guys on the team." He shoved his hands deep into his pockets. "So I told the coach to take a walk. Only . . ." He paused, then smiled a little.

"Only what?"

"Only I wasn't that polite."

I tried to see the whole thing in my mind—the coach telling Tiimo he could be the team manager and Tiimo, his pride hurt, yelling straight back into the coach's face.

"Did you feel better after you told him off?" I asked.

"At first. But I felt like an idiot later, especially when I realized Murph and a couple other guys were standing in the hall listening to everything that was going on."

I didn't say anything.

"Anyway," said Tiimo like he didn't care anymore, "I thought I had a pretty good chance to make the team this year, but I didn't. Guess I'm just not a player after all."

We sat together in silence although I could hear kids talking in the hallway. I thought about all the things Tiimo *was* good at—making little kids laugh, looking out for his mom and grandma, being a friend to Murph.

"I'm sorry you didn't make the team," I said.

Dreams. What did you do with the ones that weren't good anymore?

"Look, Gracie," Tiimo whispered, "I have to tell you something before everybody comes out here. You know that night in the park? I wanted to kiss you then."

196

The front door swung open.

"Hey, guys!" said Murph.

"I just thought you ought to know," Tiimo said in a voice that only I could hear.

chapter 19

~~~~~~~~~~ ◆

Ever since Pete told me he didn't think Mom and I were alike I'd been thinking of the ways we were different. One of the big ways, I decided, was that Mom usually avoided unpleasant things—like balancing her checkbook, for instance, or telling daughters that they were moving to Salt Lake. I don't like doing hard things either, but I do them anyway.

I woke up the morning after Jill's party, and I knew it was time for me to visit her in the hospital. I would go that night.

After dinner Sinjian sat in the bathroom with me and watched me curl my hair.

"Did you know that if you get stuck in a tornado you could get your head snapped off?" he asked.

"No," I said, "I didn't know that."

"It's true."

"Well, I guess it's a good thing we live here then," I said. "There aren't any tornadoes in Utah."

Sinjian caught my eyes in the mirror and smiled.

"Where are you going? On a date?" he asked.

"No, I am not going on a date. I'm walking to the hospital so I can see Mom."

"Oh." He thought awhile. "When is she coming home?"

I shrugged. "Pete says soon. I don't know."

Pete said Mom was getting stronger, getting better all the time. I didn't know if that were really true or if Pete just wanted it to be true.

"Wait a minute," Sinjian said. He left the room and came back a few minutes later. "Take this picture to her, okay? I drew it."

It was a picture of two ninjas kicking each other in the face. Just the sort of thing guaranteed to cheer up a sick person.

When I walked outside, I saw Mrs. Burns scurrying around her front porch. "Tatiana! Where are you?" Her voice shook.

"Come, Tatiana!"

Mrs. Burns sounded like she might cry.

"Please come home to me . . ."

I stopped. What should I do? A thought flashed through my head: *Mom would know how to handle this!*

"There you are!" Mrs. Burns gave a little laugh of relief, then bent over to scoop up Tatiana, who had been crouching behind the milk box. "You naughty girl!" She kissed Tatiana on the head, then held her close.

I let out my breath and started down the stairs.

"Gracie."

Mrs. Burns was talking to me?

"Well, that's your name isn't it?"

I stopped and faced her. "Yes. That's right."

As always, there were spongy pink curlers at the nape of her neck. Who was she curling her hair for? In all the time we'd lived here, I'd never seen anybody come to visit her. Not even once.

I started to shake.

"Your mother," she said. "How's she doing?"

"I—I don't know. I'm on my way to see her right now."

"Tell her that Ava Burns says hello."

A breeze picked up, rattling crumpled papers in the gutter. Mrs. Burns shivered, then disappeared with Tatiana into her empty house.

Mom was stretched out on her bed when I walked into the hospital room. Her dark hair was fanned out on the pillow, and her skin looked as white-gray as the moon. I could see her collarbones jutting out over the neck of her robe, she was so thin. There was a plastic bracelet with her name on her wrist.

She was sleeping.

My knees went weak with relief, and I sank into a vinyl-covered chair by the door.

I don't have to talk to her yet.

What would I say when she woke up?

Mom's room was small and clean and—except for the

single bouquet of flowers on the nightstand—totally cheerless in the way hospital rooms always are. At least she was alone. If there was anything more depressing than being crazy, I decided, it would be having to share a bedroom with someone else who was crazy, too.

I looked again at the flowers. They were a mix of carnations and daisies stuck in a mason jar. I had to smile a little. It would be just like Pete to use a fruit jar instead of a real vase, but they did brighten the place up.

Did Mom love flowers as much as I did? I didn't know. There were probably lots of things about her that I didn't really know.

I stood up, walked to the edge of her bed, and looked at her, still sleeping. Her chest rose and fell, rose and fell, full of gentle breath.

I had a memory of her and me.

Mom was standing in the living room of our old house in American Fork, holding a record in her hand, when I walked through the front door.

"Gracie! Look what I just found!"

She showed me an old Beatles album.

"My friends and I used to play this record all the time when we were little kids. We'd put it on the old hi-fi downstairs and pretend we were singing on television. We danced, too."

Mom took the record from its jacket, then put it on our stereo. The record made scratching noises at first, then music filled the air.

"This is 'Twist and Shout.' I used to *love* this song,"

she said. She started singing and dancing along with the words.

I stood in the middle of the floor watching her, my arms folded across my chest, thinking that she was being a little silly. Mom looked at me and smiled.

"Come on, come on, Gracie now!" she sang to the music.

She moved toward me, took both of my hands in hers, and began spinning me around. The room turned into circles of blurred color.

"Shake it up, Gracie now!"

I was choking out laughs and so was Mom. We went completely wild after that. We shook our arms and heads to the beat of the music.

"Hey, look at you, Gracie. You can really *move!*"

I jumped up on the couch with my shoes on and started to bounce with the music, then stopped to see what Mom would say.

She stopped singing and looked straight at me. "I'm gonna get you for that!" she said. Then she laughed again and leaped onto the couch herself, singing and jumping with me. When the song was over, we collapsed together. Mom's face was sweaty and red, and she was breathing hard.

"What a great song," she said. Then she scooped me up in her arms and kissed my cheek.

I remember every single detail about that moment— her breath on my hot face, the sound of her laugh, the bright colors of the room melting together as I twirled to the music, the prayer I said in my head.

Oh please Jesus please. This is what I want. I want her to be happy.

So I can be happy too.

I looked at Mom now, still sleeping, then looked outside the window. It was getting darker. I could see the moon already glowing and slipping from the sky through the branches of a tree like a silver coin. "I wish I could make you better," I whispered. "But I really can't."

She was a little like the moon, my mother, whole and shining sometimes. But only sometimes. Maybe it would always be that way with her.

Mom stirred at the sound of my voice, then opened her eyes. The dimmed light in them went up a little when she saw me.

"Hi," I said.

"Baby."

There was a long pause.

"So. How've you been?" A pretty stupid question.

"Okay," she said. "They try to keep us busy—talking, exercising, developing new hobbies."

"You already have a hobby," I told her. "Singing is your hobby."

She looked at me thoughtfully. "I haven't sung for a long time, Gracie. I'm probably no good anymore."

"You could sing for me now. Like you used to," I said.

She fingered the plastic bracelet nervously while her

203

eyes grew big. She was scared that she couldn't sing anymore.

I let out a deep breath, then shrugged. "No big deal."

"I'm so sorry," she said, and I knew she was apologizing for more than not singing to me. I looked out the window and said nothing.

A long time passed before she said anything.

"How are things at home?" she asked in the polite voice that strangers use with each other.

"Fine," I said in the same formal voice. Then I reached into my purse and pulled out the ninja picture. "Sinjian wants me to give this to you."

She laughed when she saw it. It was a tired, thin laugh, but it made me feel better somehow.

"I'll have to get to know him," she said.

"Yeah, well, he isn't so bad."

Another silence.

"Gracie?"

I looked at Mom and saw that her eyes were filled with quiet tears.

"Do *you* think I'll ever sing again?"

I wasn't going to lie anymore. For her. About her. To her. "I don't know. I guess that's pretty much up to you, Mom." Then I added more gently. "I hope you do."

She reached out toward me, so I took her hand and held it for a little while until it didn't feel so cold.

As I got ready to leave I saw pictures of people in my mind. Danny, the retarded man who bagged groceries at the store where Mom worked. The lady in the parking lot who'd asked for money because she had kids at home. Mrs. Burns and Tatiana.

"Mrs. Burns says hello." I paused in the doorway. "Her first name's Ava."

"Thank you," Mom said like I had given her a gift.

Danny, the lady, Mrs. Burns—Mom treats them like they count. To her, they do.

I turned out the light so she could sleep. *Someday,* I thought, *I will tell her I love that about her.*

Later, I sat on the hospital grounds for a long time, not thinking at all at first, just feeling the cool evening air wash over me—my legs, my shoulders, the top of my head—then slowly realizing that there was something I had to have.

When I scrambled to my feet, my heart was beating loudly in my own ears. I started to run, my feet making even music against the pavement.

Faster, faster.

Past the hospital, past the Medicine Shoppe on South Temple, straight on to O Street.

I passed the duplex where Tatiana was yowling from the end of her rope. I passed the house on the corner where the kids who beat up Sinjian lived. I ran right to Tiimo's house.

I gulped for air as I pounded on his door.

Tiimo answered.

"I came to collect," I announced, like I was on an official repossession.

205

Tiimo looked puzzled.

"You—you owe me a kiss," I said.

Tiimo didn't say anything, but a small surprised smile formed on his lips. He let himself out onto the front porch and looked at me. *Really* looked at me. If I hadn't already been red from running, I would have started blushing.

"Is that right?" He leaned casually against the house and folded his arms across his chest. He was smiling broadly now.

"That's right." Too late to back out now.

"What about interest? I'm a few weeks overdue," he pointed out.

I felt my legs go weak. "I came to collect interest, too."

We looked straight into each other's eyes.

"Wait here a minute, Gracie," he finally said, then disappeared into the house. When he returned he dangled a set of car keys from his hand.

"Let's go for a ride," he said.

Tiimo and I drove all over the valley. The empty fields of grass that grew along the highways were brown and yellow from the summer sun, but the trees still grew green and straight. The wind rushing through the open windows cooled my face.

"I'm going to take you to my favorite place," Tiimo said.

We drove back to the city, up Main Street, and past the old bronze statue of Brigham Young.

Tiimo pulled the car up in front of a tiny shaded park. "This is Memory Grove," he said. "See that road running up from here? That takes you through City Creek Canyon. Can you believe it? We've got a canyon right here in the middle of town. You come here and you feel like you're in another world."

Tiimo and I got out of the car and walked through the park. I could hear City Creek splashing over flat stones on its way downhill.

"I used to ride my skateboard over here whenever I needed a place to think about things." He paused. "Sometimes I imagined what it would feel like to bring a girl here with me." He reached for my hand. "Guess I'm going to find out now."

We sat on a bench surrounded by cottonwoods and didn't say a word. Tiimo ran his cool strong fingers across the base of my neck, then up into my hair.

"I'm glad you moved here, Gracie." We turned to each other then, and Tiimo kissed me until my head felt light.

chapter 20

At breakfast the next morning, Sinjian shared his favorite cereal with me—Frankenberry—and I ate it even though it turned my milk pale pink.

"What I really need is a job," I said. "I turn sixteen next week."

"I'm gonna work at a pizza store," said Sinjian. "Then I can eat all the pizza I want for free. Also people give you money for pizza and you can keep it. For reals." He stuck his arm in the cereal box. "When I get money I'll buy you a birthday present. A Barbie. The one with hair that grows."

"I'd like that," I said. He rooted around for the plastic prize at the bottom. Bits of cereal flew like popcorn onto the counter.

"Wait until the box is empty," I said. "Please."

I took another bite of cereal. This is the single worst thing I have ever eaten, I thought.

"Dad and me will make you a party."

I smiled. "Really?"

"Yeah!" He started to sing. "Happy birthday to you! You live in a zoo! You look like a monkey! And you smell like one, too!"

I laughed.

"Only you don't really look like a monkey, Gracie."

"Well," I said. "That's a relief."

HELP WANTED/ SEE MANAGER

The sign was posted in front of the Granny Goodson Cookie Counter in the mall.

"Excuse me," I said to the girl behind the counter. "I'd like to speak to the manager about a job."

He was tall and skinny, with pale skin and dark hair. He wore a white shirt, plaid vest, and bow tie—the Granny Goodson uniform. His name plate said DIRK. "What can I do for you?" he asked.

"My name's Gracie Davis. I wanted to find out about your job opening."

"What kind of employment experience do you have?"

"I—I haven't had a regular job before except baby-sitting and some housecleaning."

Dirk looked bored.

"I make good cookies though," I said.

Dirk laughed. "A bum off the street can make good cookies here. Tight production control."

"Oh," I said, suddenly feeling like a fool. Why did I think I could ever get a job in the first place? I didn't have any experience—

"Can you work on Friday nights?"

"Sure," I gulped. "Of course."

"Fine. Why don't you fill out an application, and we'll see you tomorrow."

By the time I left Granny Goodson, a uniform tucked beneath my arm, I wanted to sing, whistle, even slide down corridors in my stocking feet I felt so good. I had a job!

I was humming when I passed Busy Bee Toys. I paused, then went inside the store.

She was still there.

Amelia.

I dropped down to see her.

Her black curls lay soft against the blue velvet of her cape and the bright skates dangled from her hand.

I looked at Amelia long and hard, remembering how beautiful I used to think she was, and then when nobody was looking, I kissed the tips of my fingers and pressed them against the glass.

epilogue

~~~~~~~~~~~~~~~~~~ ◆

.

It's fall now.

Salt Lake City is actually a very beautiful place this time of year. During September the tops of the mountains, where it's coldest first, turn red and gold. Then the colors start chasing like flames down the hillside and finally into the valley so that the box elder trees that line my street look like huge torches of swirling light.

I love the way that the street is starting to feel like home to me.

Mom is back. She takes her medicine and goes on long walks with Pete every morning before he goes to work. She's talking about finding a job herself but says she isn't ready just yet.

I haven't heard her sing.

Sinjian is still with us. Lily called at the end of the summer to ask if he wanted to join her, but he said "Gracie needs me," if you can believe it. He started first grade at Wasatch Elementary a few weeks ago, and every morning I fix him a sack lunch to take because he says that school lunch sucks.

At night Mom reads to Sinjian, whose favorite poem is "Jabberwocky." When she says the lines "One, two! One, two! And through and through— The vorpal blade went snicker-snack!" Sinjian leaps to his feet and slices the air with his arm.

Occasionally Pete talks about getting his Americalife business going—naturally he still has all the posters and products stacked in the corner of his room—but he doesn't sound too excited about it anymore. I think he actually likes his job downtown. They've been giving him more responsibility because it turns out he has a knack for computers.

Me, I started my junior year, and things are going okay considering the fact I'm new. The classes are maybe a little harder, and sometimes I'll notice that my clothes aren't quite right or that I say things differently. But Jill has helped a lot. She's friendly with everybody, something I really respect. Most kids don't even say "hi" to people who aren't in their own group.

Tiimo and I spend a lot of time together—at school and after. He teases me by saying that he couldn't play football even if he were on the team because I take up too much of his time.

"Oh yeah?" I say. "You spend more time with the kids on your team than you ever do with me."

Tiimo is coaching a soccer team for four- to six-year-olds, and, yes, Sinjian is playing.

That's what I'm doing right this very minute, as a matter of fact. I'm sitting on a blanket, watching a bunch of little kids trying to kick the ball, but mostly kicking each other in the shins instead.

"That's the way, Willy," Tiimo calls to one of the kids from the sidelines. "Dribble the ball. Take it all the way down the field."

Murph stands by Tiimo, arms folded and legs spread apart. *"I repeat,"* he screams, *"take no prisoners!"*

Sinjian is on the field, wearing his blue shorts and yellow jersey which he thinks are even better than ninja clothes. He sleeps in his uniform the night before a game so he'll be ready to play.

The only problem so far is that Sinjian never makes actual contact with the ball. It's like there's a force field around the ball that keeps Sinjian exactly five feet away from it at any given moment.

"Let's go you guys!" I yell and clap. "You can do it!"

The ball squirts loose from a pack of kids and rolls straight toward Sinjian.

I leap to my feet. "Kick it! Kick it!"

He moves toward the ball in slow motion, shuffling his feet across the carpet of grass. I hear Tiimo's voice. "Go for it, Sinjian!"

Sinjian approaches the ball, cocks back his leg, then lets loose with a mighty kick. He barely skims the top of the ball with his foot before falling flat on his back.

"Good try, pal!" yells Tiimo.

Sinjian scrambles to his feet again and scans the sidelines until he sees me.

"Hey, Gracie!" he screams from the field. "Hey, Gracie, did you see that goal I almost scored?!"

"Yeah! It was great!"

I look over at Tiimo to see if he's heard Sinjian. Tiimo
is staring at me, grinning. He waves at me to join him.
When I do, he puts his arm around my shoulders.

"That kid is a real case," he says. We look right at each
other. And laugh.

"He's crazy. It—it runs in our family."

It feels good to be able to say something like that, a
little joke.

"Tiimo! Tiimo!" One of the little kids calls. "Erin fell
down. I think she sprained her head."

Tiimo pulls a face at me. "Don't leave."

I watch him run out to the field, squat down by Erin,
check her head, say something that makes her laugh
even though she's still crying.

Leave?

I can't think of a single other place I want to be.

about the author

A. E. CANNON credits the beginning of her writing career to a childhood illness that put her in bed for a year. "I had strict instructions from our doctor —no walking, no running, no swimming, no biking. With nothing else to do, I was forced to discover books. Before I knew it, books moved into my life permanently, setting up house and lounging around in chairs and on the foot of my bed just like a crowd of favorite cousins. They introduced me to people who had tea parties on the ceiling and others who went down rabbit holes. I eventually got better, but I asked the books to stay anyway. They did."

Her first novel, *Cal Cameron by Day, Spider-Man™ by Night*, won the Fifth Annual Delacorte Press Prize for an Outstanding First Young Adult Novel. Her second, *The Shadow Brothers*, was chosen as a Best Book for Young Adults by the American Library Association.

She lives with her husband and sons and their many pets in Salt Lake City.